The *Literary* Thread

An Elizabeth Grant Mystery

Ginette Guy Mayer

Ginette Guy Mayer

2

This book is a work of fiction. References to real people, events, establishments, organizations, or locales are intended only to provide a sense of authenticity and are used fictitiously. All other characters, incidents, and dialogue are drawn from the author's imagination and are not to be constructed as real.

www.ginetteguymayer.com

Cover design by Ginette Guy Mayer
Using Postermywall.com

ISBN 978-1-7380450-0-6 (Paperback)
ISBN 978-1-7380450-1-3 (eBook)
ISBN-978-1-7380450-2-0 (Large Print Paperback)

Contents

Ginette Guy Mayer

Acknowledgement

A big thank you to Paul R. King for keeping a keen eye on the commas and the dots. And, for his encouragement with this project.

Thank you to all the characters in this book who think nothing of waking me up at 4 am because they have something clever to say.

Books in the Elizabeth Grant series

A Peculiar Case from the Files of Elizabeth Grant

The Gale

The Literary Thread

Other books by Ginette Guy

Unforgotten Mary Mack Cornwall's First Lady

Books available in French

Inoubliable Mary Mack

Un Cas Particulier

La Tourmente

Prologue

Muriel was sitting cross-legged on her mother's bed, watching her pack. Helpfully, or so she thought, commenting and critiquing every piece of clothing Elizabeth was putting in the suitcase.

"So, where are you going?" asked Muriel.

"We're not telling anyone, it's a vacation, a time away," replied Elizabeth. "Only Peter knows. So even before you think about harassing him, I trained him, and he won't tell. After everything that's happened, it will be nice for Harry and me to have some quiet time."

"Country? City? By what you are packing I don't think you're going to a cabin," said Muriel. "Don't take that skirt it's not your best. What about shoes? Do you have anything new?"

"We are gone just over a week. I don't need too many things. Should we do some walking, I want comfortable shoes, leave it alone."

Muriel took it upon herself to fill the other side of the suitcase with her own selection. It was June but the nights could still be cool, so she added sweaters. "In the city then, dinners? Do you need something better like the dress you wore for the Chateau Laurier dinner?" asked Muriel. "What about nightgowns? You're not bringing that flannel thing grandma wore, are you? You'll come back single if you do that!" exclaimed Muriel.

Elizabeth took out most of the things that Muriel had shoved in the case and slammed it shut.

"What are you going to do while you're in town?" asked Elizabeth.

"Thanks for letting me stay here for the two weeks," replied Muriel who was on assignment with The Ottawa Journal. "I jumped at the chance to cover Cornwall while our regular reporter is away. I will keep everything clean and I will remember to feed the cat. Also, I will help Julie and Peter renovate the café. It will be lovely when it's finished."

"Yes, they are working hard," said Elizabeth. "It was a wonderful opportunity for Julie to buy that coffee shoppe with its convenient location. It was a perfect use of the money she received from her mother."

"I think that's it," said Muriel.

Muriel reached into her own suitcase and took out a book. "Here, I'll loan you this book. It's a new writer, nobody had heard of her before and still now that the book is a best-seller, she remains completely out of the public eye. You might have time to read it if you're bringing that nightgown!"

Elizabeth made a face at her and Muriel threw in the latest novel by J.S. Simmons, *Spies and Innuendos*, and closed the case.

Chapter 1

Harry was waiting downstairs in the cab that would take them to the train station. They both laughed at the excitement of getting away from their busy Cornwall lives even if it was only for a short break. Elizabeth ran her private investigation agency and Harry had a car dealership and garage. Both were on the good side of the fifty mark and their relationship was new but it had been marked by challenges. Harry's estranged wife was killed by the mob and he had found a daughter in the process. The stress had no doubt caused his heart attack earlier in the year. Elizabeth and her business partner in Montreal had been key in solving the case, bringing some of the criminal elements to justice. Elizabeth was comfortable with the professional and personal choices she had made.

Both were exhausted, beyond physical tiredness, from trying to keep it all together for the sake of Harry's children and family. He suggested some time away, a mini vacation, something he couldn't remember ever doing. Harry first mentioned a cabin in the woods and some fishing. Elizabeth didn't dislike the idea but since it was June, swarms of black flies and mosquitoes came to mind. With no indoor plumbing and facilities, the prospect of cooking and cleaning did not look like much of a vacation to her.

They settled for the city, and a short escape by train to Toronto was the winning destination. Harry loved music, he had been taught piano by his mother and was quite good. They selected a few concerts and dinner venues. Harry would take an afternoon to visit a friend who also had a garage while Elizabeth went shopping. Her friend Mary had recommended a few shows and that completed the program.

They chose not to tell anyone where they were going in part because they knew they had trusted people to help fill in during their absence. Elizabeth had hired her nephew Peter Darvis a few years back and her partner, François Lefebvre could help if needed. His office was in the southwest area of Montreal, in Lachine, and staffed with a secretary and freelance investigator. They could look after things there if he needed to come to Cornwall. The only person who knew they were going to The Royal York was Peter, in case of any emergencies. Her daughter recently had a baby and Harry's father was in his seventies and living with him. Julie, his daughter, was going to stay with her grandfather while they were away.

"This is nice," said Harry. "I can't remember the last time I just looked out a window and watched the world go by. I'm looking forward to that *Hart House String Quartet* concert."

"Yes, Mary told me about them," said Elizabeth. "Did you know that Boris Hambourg from the group came to Cornwall to see her? She was thinking of booking them for the Arts Association concert season. I'm not sure what came of it."

They settled in for the journey with a cup of hot coffee. Elizabeth was deep in thought when Harry asked, "What is it? You look worried."

"Are we going to be all right?" she asked.

Harry was surprised by the question because he had never heard her be anything but confident, outwardly anyway. This was a mark of trust that she was willing to share what was on her mind.

"Of course, it will be. The kids are doing fine. You have a beautiful and healthy new grandson. I couldn't be happier that Peter is helping Julie with the café."

"No, I mean us, you and me. This will be the first time we are spending so much time together, on our own," said Elizabeth, with some concern in her voice.

"We survived hurricane Maureen. How bad could anything else be?" Maureen had been Harry's estranged wife. She had brought chaos and danger into their lives before passing away recently.

"What I mean is the day-to-day stuff. It's the petty things that drive people apart. Do you know why fairy tales always end with *They lived happily ever after*? Because they don't want to deal with them sharing a bathroom and getting on each other's nerves over toilet seats and messy toothbrushes."

"I promise you I won't let a toothbrush come between us," laughed Harry.

"We're not young anymore, we are set in our ways," said Elizabeth. "You have spent most of your life alone, and I can be fiercely independent and a bit stubborn. Prince Charming might not be so ready to share his closet space when he finds out Cinderella is all clutter and chaos."

"I'm sure we can talk things through before resentment sets in. Prince Charming isn't called charming for nothing," said Harry as he kissed her hand.

The weather was good all week. The warmer days of June brought out flowers and birds. On the first morning, Elizabeth woke up to find Harry sitting in the chair next to the bed, all dressed and looking at her. The second morning, he was still sitting in the chair, but in his robe. Finally, on the third day, he relaxed and slept in. They went for walks, discovered restaurants and shops, they filled in the space with conversation, but even the silences were comfortable.

On Thursday, Harry went to see his friend in town. Elizabeth decided to fill in the time with some shopping and got back to the hotel early enough to relax and start the book that Muriel had loaned her. She glanced over the title and *Spies and Innuendos* seemed a little too much like business to her, but she dove in anyway. It was good and she couldn't put it down. Getting into the storyline, she realized it was oddly familiar. One of the supporting characters was a lawyer, working for his country's defence department. His work involved international affairs and at present a communist plot to infiltrate the political scene. The lawyer was killed under suspicious conditions, a car crash on a countryside road.

Elizabeth went white as the sheets and dropped the book on her lap. She picked it up again and looked at the dust cover. Title and description, reviews and best seller's list but no author's biography or photos. She looked at the name again, J.S. Simmons and gasped. She remembered the envelope she received last fall, after that peculiar case. It contained a memoir of sorts from Josephine Smith, a spy and informant herself, who was at the centre of the book theft with Fenian connections. She remembered placing the memoirs in her safe, without even looking at them.

She had only read the note attached:

Keep this safe for me; I trust you to know if and when it might be needed. Josephine Smith.

Elizabeth never quite understood why Josephine had entrusted her with the manuscript. Josephine had tried to shoot her. Fortunately, the gun misfired and afterwards set her office on fire with her in it. Harry had saved her and Josephine disappeared after going to London for questioning. The envelope that contained the memoirs had a return address of Saint-Lunaire in France and the name was J.S. Simmons. Elizabeth had never told anyone about this.

She read the pages again that related to the lawyer's accident and realized it was about her husband. Every detail was significant and accurate. He had been a lawyer for the Canadian Department of Justice in Ottawa. That's how they had met when she had a temporary assignment from the typing pool to his office. He worked on international affairs and they had worked together on the Fenian Brotherhood's involvement in Canada. Four years ago, he died in a car crash on a country road. She had never associated the possibility that his work might have caused his demise. Thoughts and feelings swirled around in her mind. Could it be right?

She took the hotel stationery and wrote to Edward Rushton, a colleague and friend of her husband. He still worked for the Department of Justice. They had collaborated last year when that Josephine Smith saga came along. She mentioned the book and her suspicions. He could investigate it and see whether she was being rational about it all. She went down to the lobby and dropped the letter in the outgoing mailbox. Harry walked in while she was waiting for the elevator back to the room.

"Hi, did you have a nice visit with your friend?" she asked.

"Wonderful, he has a huge dealership, of course being Toronto," he replied. "We talked about old times and I also filled him in on recent events. I got some clever ideas about things I can do for sales in Cornwall. You?"

"I went shopping and got some things you might like, otherwise I relaxed," replied Elizabeth as they entered their room. She didn't mention the book, she was trying to push it out of her mind. At least until she heard back from Rushton. Time was too precious and she didn't want to waste it on Josephine Smith.

"Edgar loaned me a car for a few days," he said with a big grin on his face. "And…he is loaning us his cottage on Lake Simcoe. If you kiss me, I'll give you the keys to the cottage…I'm keeping the keys to the boat house and the convertible of course!"

She graciously complied with the request and within an hour she had claimed all the keys for herself. "Good thing I bought a bathing suit."

They headed out of the city early the next morning and stopped for a short break and coffee. Elizabeth suggested they pick up a few supplies for meals before leaving.

"It's very nice of your friend to let us use his place," said Elizabeth. "Is it a family cottage?"

"No, not really," replied Harry. "I think it's more a business asset. He loans it to clients and colleagues. I don't think he goes there much himself; he does throw a few parties in season."

"Have you been there?" asked Elizabeth.

"Yes, only once and I left before the weekend was over," replied Harry. "Edgar is married, but he likes the ladies. His wife got tired of that and now they live parallel lives. His parties are well-known for being a little different."

Elizabeth was now curious. "I'm learning about your wild days. Why did you leave early?"

"I had gone up with a lady friend, and of course, Edgar showed an interest in her. I don't like to share what I bring," he said coyly.

"Oh, I see…" she said.

"I'm going to put the top down on the convertible now that it's warmer. Do you want to drive?" he asked.

"YES. Those keys are mine, remember…" Her smile widened and she said, "How fast can I go in that candy-red model?"

"Now, now, it's a loaner," warned Harry. He knew that some of his friends didn't let their wives drive or allowed them a licence. But for him, raised on a farm, everyone drove, his mother, his sisters. They drove all the machinery and the trucks; it was a necessity. He enjoyed seeing Elizabeth have fun.

They arrived in Innisfil and made their way to the lakeside. Edgar's place was on a private road lined with a row of upscale cottages, all facing the water. Elizabeth was impressed. This was no fishing cabin! They entered the circular drive to gaze at the two-storey main building. At the centre was a turret entry with a one-storey wing on the right. It was huge. The wrap-around veranda leads to the waterfront view. Only the wood shingles betrayed that this was a country home. There were two rocking chairs on the corner of the veranda. If they were going to look like an old couple, this was the place to do it!

The interior was comfortable with exposed beams and a wood stove in the kitchen. She hoped the evening would be cool enough to light a fire in the large stone fireplace. Upstairs in the main bedroom, the bed faced large windows with a breathtaking view of the lake.

Elizabeth noticed Harry had disappeared to the boat house and the door was open. In it sat a gleaming twenty-one foot all mahogany Chris Craft runabout. The fifty-year-old reverted to a boy as he turned the key and said, "Listen to that!"

Chapter 2

Muriel was at her mother's desk, typing her latest article for *The Ottawa Journal.* The newspaper coverage of events in Cornwall was quite extensive. They had articles on local politics, sports and social events. This temporary assignment was a chance for Muriel to prove herself. Up to now she mostly did copy editing but she was eager for more. It was hard in 1934 to push through as a woman reporter. Most women who wrote were limited to affairs of the heart, social columns and obituaries. Few covered the major stories, but that's where she wanted to be one day.

The door opened and in walked a tall man, good-looking, with a suit that fitted so well, it looked tailor-made. He looked to be in his thirties, with brown hair and a dashing smile.

"Hi, I'm looking for Peter Darvis. I'm François Lefebvre, his colleague from Montreal," he said.

"Oh, hi. I'm Muriel Grant, Elizabeth's daughter. "It's nice to meet you, I've heard a lot about you. And thank you for helping Harry."

Muriel was in her twenties with light-coloured hair in a fashionable wave. François did not see a physical resemblance to Elizabeth but he noticed they shared the same light in their eyes.

"I'm glad that things are quieter for both of them now and that they could get away for a bit of a break," he said. "I'm here to work with Peter on a couple of cases today and tomorrow, probably."

"Peter is at his friend Julie's café, they are updating the look before the opening. I can take you over there if you want?"

"I don't want to disturb you, I see you are working," said Lefebvre.

"No bother at all, I'm finishing an article I'm sending to *The Ottawa Journal.* I'm a journalist there." Muriel thought that was not technically accurate, but for the next ten days anyway, she was a reporter.

François was an ex-police officer before opening his detective agency. He had been forced to retire due to an injury that left him with a slight limp. He had known journalists, some better and some worse, but no women had covered vice and organized crime where he worked.

"If you have the time to take me over, that would be great. Thank you," said Lefebvre.

Julie had taken over *The Cornwall Coffee Shoppe* at 23 Second Street East. She was giving it a good scrub and new décor going for a Cornwall vintage feel. Elizabeth had suggested the theme using old photos. Julie had enjoyed working at MacDonald's Diner next door and having her own place would give her independence and security for the future. The inheritance money had come from her mother, gained illegally from her connections to the Montreal mob. So, it had not been taken easily. But part of the money was given to the local orphanage and she was trying to put the rest to good use.

When Muriel and François walked into the café, Julie and Peter were reviewing paint samples and supply catalogues. The place was very much a work in progress.

"Hi. I'm sorry François, I should have been in the office, but time flew by," said Peter. He introduced Julie who walked right over, took his arm and thanked him for helping them. Lefebvre had been the first one to find reports of her in foster care and deal with her mother's mob connections.

"You're welcome, I'm glad to meet you," said Lefebvre. "This is going to be nice, congratulations."

"Thank you. I'm planning to offer breakfast and a light lunch. I will be hiring a cook and we will focus on good coffee and desserts too."

"In Montreal, the spots with fancy coffees and hot chocolates are becoming popular," said Lefebvre. "I'm sure you will do well. Can you show me the kitchen?" François wanted to talk to her in a more private area.

"I'm sorry about your mother," he said. "I knew her from my days with the Montreal police."

"Thanks, she was a colourful character, to say the least," said Julie sadly. "I had long stopped believing she could ever change."

"With that in mind would you like to help someone else who is willing to change?" asked François. "I have kept in touch with some of the ladies in my old beat. My secretary is one of those women who wanted a switch in trade if you know what I mean."

"Yes, I do," said Julie. "How can I help?"

"Giving someone a hand up maybe," he said. "I know you are looking for a breakfast cook, and I know just the woman. She has experience as a cook in a lumber camp before coming to Montreal years ago. Once in the big city, with no friends, she made the wrong choice in a difficult situation. A small town and a new outlook would make a world of difference for her, I'm sure."

"That could work," said Julie. "I was reluctant to take my mother's money, but Elizabeth convinced me I could also do some good with it. So that would go along with that thinking."

"Great. I will let Peter know and you can arrange to talk to her. Thank you," said François as they rejoined the others.

"I'll stay and help Julie for a while," said Muriel. "So, Peter can get back to the office."

"François is staying in town tonight," said Peter. "Do you want to have dinner with us? Julie will bring her grandfather since he is all alone at the house."

"That would be fun," said Muriel. "See you tonight."

They worked all afternoon and only stopped to get the paint off their hands and change for dinner. They would go to the King George dining room since that was where François was staying.

Julie picked up her grandfather John. "Are you sure you want me to come?" he asked. "You're a bunch of young people, I can manage here you know."

"Nonsense, grandfather. You're as young in your outlook as anyone I ever met," said Julie. "Plus, you need to meet François, he was such a big help and you know everyone else."

The five of them had a wonderful time, exchanging stories and laughing. They learned a bit more about François's work and past experiences with the police. Muriel was eager to ask questions about some of the cases he and Peter had dealt with in Montreal.

"Anything going on now, that I could write about?" Muriel asked. "I would love to cover a sensational story, put my name on the article."

François laughed, she reminded him of Elizabeth and how eager she had been to prove herself as an investigator and put her name on the door of the office. Muriel was an attractive woman, an ambitious journalist and Elizabeth's daughter. The combination was a triple threat that scared him more than some of the mobsters he had encountered.

The next morning Muriel opted to let Peter and François work without disruption. She had been a little too free with the wine the night before and opted for coffee at Julie's. When she walked in Julie looked distraught.

"What's up?" asked Muriel. "It's a lot of work but give me strong coffee and I'll help."

"Coming right up," said Julie. "I should have

paid more attention in school, that's what I'm finding out."

Muriel knew that Julie had spent time in foster care and moved around a lot before finding good foster parents in Williamstown. Harry's estranged wife had never told him about his daughter.

"It's normal to be a bit overwhelmed, but you'll get it all done," said Muriel. "There's a lot of people to support you now."

"Yes, I know and I'm glad for it," said Julie. "Your mother has been good in making me believe I could do this. And Peter, with his accounting training, is helping me with the numbers and that part of the business."

"What can I do?" asked Muriel.

"Well, you're good with words and writing, can you look at the menus for me?" asked Julie. "I'm not changing the name of the place; people know it as such. I want to open early, do a good breakfast and have mid-morning coffee, tea and pastries. A lot of it will be to go, for the people that are working."

"And what about lunches?" asked Muriel. "You said soups and sandwiches, nothing too complicated?"

"You got it. I used to work at MacDonald's next door and Duncan has been good about me opening something right beside him. But he does full meals and opens later, so there is not too much competition."

"That was thoughtful of you. Ok, let me see what you have so far and I can put something together. We can look at doing a little ad for the paper, to announce the opening."

"Perfect. Thank you so much," said Julie.

They kept busy all morning, only stopping for lunch. Mid-afternoon, Muriel decided to go back to the office and see if she could bother Peter for some leads on interesting stories in town.

François was getting ready to leave when she came into the office. Again today, he was wearing a well-tailored suit with a stylish tie, a blue art deco with swirls. "It was nice to meet you, Miss Grant," he said. "I look forward to reading your articles."

"Thank you. Our paths may cross again. We have a lot of friends in common now," said Muriel.

When Peter closed the door behind François, he turned back to Muriel and teased, "Our paths may cross again!" "What's up with that?"

"Never mind," said Muriel. "So, any interesting stories I can work on?"

"1934 is the 150th anniversary of the town. There is a lot planned for this summer. That's interesting."

"No, I'm talking about murders, crimes, smuggling…Some of the stuff you and Mother work on all the time."

"You could go over to the court building and see what cases are coming to trial," he said. "Otherwise for community issues, you could talk to Mary Randolph, your mother's friend. She is with the Federated Charities and they deal with social and women's issues."

"All good ideas, thanks. I went over to help Julie this morning, I'm doing the design for the menu and an ad for the opening."

"Thanks for doing that," said Peter. "I forget sometimes how hard things can be for her. She didn't grow up with a family around her like we did. I might have taken mine for granted."

"Things will be better now, she knows it," said Muriel. "So, where's the phone book? Where's Mary Randolph's number?"

Chapter 3

Mary agreed to meet Muriel at Fullerton's Tea Room, at the corner of Pitt and Second Street. The tearoom was one of Elizabeth's and Mary's favourite places to discuss their community involvement and other projects. Muriel had already taken a table when Mary came in. Based on her mother's description, Muriel recognized her straight away. Mary was in her mid-thirties, impeccably dressed, her hair in a wave and there was a touch of elegance about her. Her eyes reflected both intelligence and determination.

Muriel waved her over. "Hi, thank you, Miss Randolph, for agreeing to meet me."

"I'm sure I'm going to enjoy our meeting," said Mary. "I've heard a lot about you and the career of an aspiring female journalist will be enlightening, I'm sure."

"Aspiring is the word," said Muriel. "I'm doing copy editing and getting coffee more than I wish to but I'm working hard to push through."

"Yes, women often do…working twice as hard

as men to get half as far!" Mary added.

"*The Ottawa Journal* sent me to cover Cornwall for the two weeks our regular reporter is away. I'm taking this as an opportunity. Perhaps I can get one or two good stories. Peter told me you were right in the centre of things!"

"I am fortunate to be able to do a lot of community work, so I'm involved with different groups," said Mary.

"Yes, my mother tells me of some of the things you are engaged in, like the arts and charities. So, what is going on in town about which I could write?" asked Muriel.

"Well, it is the hundred and fiftieth anniversary of the town. So, this summer we have a lot of events planned. It is viewed as a "reunion" of sorts for some former residents. Now some are advertising it as "The Old Boys" reunion and as you might expect I'm not a strong supporter of that slogan!" added Mary.

"You'd think that without the "Old Girls" there wouldn't be that many old boys around!" laughed Muriel.

"Exactly! So now more advertising is coming out under the "Old Boys and Girls" Reunion. A small victory," says Mary. "I have a complete program here, so that might help you focus on certain aspects if you want. I'd be happy to add any information you may want."

"Great, thank you. I must say that as a copy editor, I have come across your name in our newspaper," said Muriel.

"Ah, yes," laughed Mary. "They like to mention the visits I make to friends in Ottawa and some functions I attend. I expect they use that when it is an otherwise slow news day!"

"It might be under the social pages, but if I may be so bold, the circles you are in, are not common for most, rarer still for the women in Cornwall." Muriel had read about dinners and balls with the Governor General and Mary's leadership in some provincial organizations.

"I can see you will make a great reporter," laughed Mary. "Some of the social connections were extended from friends of my mother. She went to a private school in Montreal, where ladies from good families were taught skills to help support a future husband's career and aspirations. They, of course, could not hope for a career of their own. She remained friends with many who are now in Ottawa, with husbands in politics, government and business."

"I know that both your grandfathers were in business and politics, but that only opens doors. It takes one's own abilities and intelligence to grow those opportunities into lasting friendships," said Muriel.

"Are you working on anything else on the community welfare front?" asked Muriel. "My mother mentioned some housing issues and other concerns."

"Yes, some years ago, the mayor suggested taking all the volunteer organizations, church groups and such, and forming them into one that would fundraise and coordinate the needs centrally," explained Mary. "The Federated Charities was then established. I'm their secretary now. Given the financial hardship of the depression, the movement from the countryside to the town, the pressures for housing and jobs have been great."

"My mother talked about some of the home visits you make, to assess the needs," said Muriel. "She says it has been eye-opening and heartbreaking."

"Yes, because we are only a group of volunteers, we have no training or structure to offer the services that are needed," said Mary. "We see the hardship and it is more than what a casual visit can fix. We would need trained social workers, with an office and administration, case files and follow-up."

"Can the Town Council not support that?" asked Muriel.

"This community has a history of supporting each other, people get involved, and the various churches support their own," explained Mary. "But now it is close to the breaking point. In the last ten years, the population grew by about fifty per cent. We are fortunate to have strong industries, but they cannot keep pace. There is no decent housing left for people coming into town."

"So, what are you going to do?" asked Muriel, jotting down notes.

"I would like to bring the issues to the political table, and ask other government levels for help," said Mary. "The issues are complex. Men with no jobs often drink more, families cramped in poor housing get sicker, youth have no activities, and the financial stress creates situations ripe for abuse. And of course, some unsavoury characters will profit from those situations."

"People are slow to act generally. We have similar issues in Ottawa," said Muriel.

"I also see the need to rally some of the men behind our objectives, to bring women's concerns to the forefront, which is not always easy. If you look at the local papers, a lot of it is about prosperity, investment, jobs and factory expansions. Sometimes people don't want to see the other side of it."

"I will put something together and see if we can get it published," said Muriel. "I want to thank you very much for taking the time, Miss Randolph."

"Any time, and please call me Mary. Let me know if you need more information or want to talk to other people. I look forward to seeing your work."

Muriel almost ran back to the office, her head full of ideas and questions. Peter was doing some paperwork and reports on cases. She practically fell into the chair across from his desk.

"What are you working on? Anything I can report on?" asked Muriel.

"No, you know you can't write on cases that are ongoing," said Peter. "There is a reason it's called a PRIVATE investigation."

"I was talking to Mary and it was very informative," she said. "We talked about poor housing and living conditions, I remember my mother mentioning it."

"Yes, we did have a few cases, for the town, gathering information, mostly about shady landlords," said Peter. "Do you want to see it?"

"Sure, let's go!" Muriel was already halfway out the door before Peter could grab the car keys. He was sure she needed to lay off the caffeine for a while.

The Town of Cornwall was defined as a perfect one-square-mile area. The boundary streets east to west were Marlborough to Cumberland, and north to south were Ninth down to Water. Water Street was canal and factories, east was the French area on Montreal Road and Highway No. 2 with more industries. Second and Pitt Streets were the main commercial areas downtown and Montreal Road in the east end.

Peter took her to the outskirts up on Cumberland. He explained that Cornwall did not have one recognized slum area but rather a few spots of inferior housing scattered here and there. The first place he showed her was about twenty feet long by ten feet wide, a two-storey, one-door structure. The second floor had a few windows but it was hard to see how they would open. Aside from the door, the only opening to let light in was at the end, high up where the first and second floors meet. The wooden boards were mismatched and it looked like the upper floor was slanted, like a box over a box.

"The town asked us to investigate some of the housing stock. When people are not working, they get a little money from the town relief fund. Because there are few places to rent, the prices have been going up and some have taken advantage," explained Peter.

"How so?" asked Muriel.

"Some had to sell their homes when the

depression hit. People with more money bought them as rental units. Some converted their garages and even sheds to rent, said Peter. "What we saw is sad, and it's the same findings with Mary and the Federated Charities' volunteers doing home visits."

Peter stopped by the side of the road and went on, "Families living in single rooms, or in shacks with no foundation, no real plumbing and no conveniences. Garages rent for $5.00 to $8.00 a month.

"We saw a family of seven in a converted garage. The mother was about to go into labour. No shade, a flat roof on a low room, and no windows that opened. It was about a hundred degrees in there. There was a row of outside toilets by their front door."

"What your mother and I reported was that some people were taken advantage of, and that's hard to fix. There are no by-laws or standards for housing at the town level. In one case the house we saw had been divided into three units, one for the owner and two for tenants. There was no water, toilet or bath in the rentals. The place had no cellar, no way to properly heat it and there were bugs. The tenants paid $5.00 and $8.00 each per month, while the taxes on the property were $13.73 for the year."

"This is so sad," said Muriel. "I can see why Mary wants to get help with this."

"Aunt Liz had tears in her eyes, and she got angry," said Peter. "Want to see a last one downtown, before we go back to the office?

"We were surprised that this was downtown, I expected better. People in and out of shops and stores all day, oblivious to the rest," said Peter. "Another family of seven, over a lean-to at the rear of a store. The floor was about a foot below ground. The wallpaper was wet, and it was summer! They had one single faucet, a toilet shared with other families."

"I've seen enough, Peter. We can go back to the office. I have articles to write," said Muriel.

Chapter 4

The vacation had gone by too fast. Elizabeth and Harry were now on their way back to reality. They opted to drop off the car at Edgar's dealership on Adelaide Street and then make their way to Union Station.

The showroom was large and bright and was clearly a success. Harry introduced her to Edgar and she thanked him for the use of the car and the cottage. Elizabeth would not have called him handsome but he certainly was tall, dark and charming. She wondered what proportion of his sales were to widows and spinsters with an expectation that the service would be above and beyond.

Edgar grasped Elizabeth's hand in both of his and assured her she was most welcome, at any time.

"Harry, how did you manage to gain the affection of such a lovely lady?" Edgar asked.

Before Harry could reply, Elizabeth untangled her hand and rested it on Harry's arm. Smiling she added, "It was all me, when I saw the value of the man, I shamelessly pursued him until he had no choice but to say yes."

"Lucky man. I'll have one of my drivers take you to the station if you want," said Edgar. "You should think about coming up to one of my summer parties. I'll send you both an invite."

On the way to the station, Harry laughed and said, "So you pursued me? I hadn't seen it that way before."

"Oh, yes, me playing hard to get was all a scheme," she said.

As usual Union Station was busy. They boarded early and Elizabeth was particularly quiet.

"I am looking forward to getting back to work, I enjoy my work," said Harry. "But I have to admit I was rather enjoying having you around all the time." Harry was hoping Elizabeth would share a similar feeling, but nothing…

"What's up?" he asked. "You are strangely quiet and that's never good, as experience has shown me."

"Do you know that book I was reading? The spy novel?" asked Elizabeth. "There is something strange about it."

"How so? Too much like recent work?" he asked.

"I think Josephine Smith wrote it," she said.

"You're not serious! Why would you think that?" said Harry curiously.

"Well…I didn't mention it before…but…She

sent me a manuscript, once the case was over. It came from a J.S. Simmons, which is the name of the author."

"I don't like the sound of that, but please go on," mumbled Harry. "Where are the papers she sent you? And what's in the book that makes you think it's hers?"

"I put the manuscript in my safe, I didn't even look at it, to be honest. I wanted to move on and forget the whole thing," said Elizabeth. "But when I read the novel, there are things in there that are unsettling. Similarities to the work my husband was doing and even the mention of that character killed in an automotive accident."

Harry took her hand and said "I'm sorry if it brought back sad memories, but how can you be sure it's her? How did you come to get the book, was it random?"

"Muriel loaned it to me, I will have to ask her," replied Elizabeth. "But on Wednesday I did write to Edward Ashton, you met him last year. I asked him to investigate it. There might be a reply letter at home."

"Now, I regret our vacation not being longer," said Harry. "But whatever it is, you need to figure it out, for your peace of mind. And mine, of course, I will worry again."

"I'm sorry Harry. This time I will tell you everything as I go," said Elizabeth.

Harry considered what was best for him, knowing everything versus knowing very little. Tough choice. The wild card here was Elizabeth herself and what rash decision she would make when the fork in the road presented itself.

Most men he talked to were concerned about their wives overspending or having mood swings. Harry on the other hand worried about Elizabeth getting in the line of fire, making deals with mobsters, or breaking into a smuggler's house. She was a grandmother for heaven's sake, not that he would dare to mention it or even hint at reigning in her free spirit. Any such attempt would relegate him to long evenings playing checkers with his father.

They arrived back in Cornwall by late afternoon and Harry called a cab to pick them up.

"Do you want to come for dinner?" he asked. "I'm sure Mrs. Denny made extra. Julie is staying with my father and I'm sure he invited Peter and Muriel most nights."

"That might be a good idea," replied Elizabeth. "I don't know what's in the cupboards. Muriel wasn't home much, I bet."

"It would also give us a chance to catch up with everyone all at once. Plus, I had a wonderful time, I can't see just letting you out of the cab and waving goodbye yet," said Harry. Elizabeth agreed.

Harry was right, although Mrs. Denny, his housekeeper had left for the day, there was a roast in the oven, vegetables and various pies. She was not put out by the extra work. She had kept house for Harry for over twenty years now and the work has been light. It had either been Harry and his son until he left for the Air Force or Harry and his father in recent years. Mrs. Denny thought it was much easier to cook for many than a few and she had no worries about leftovers.

Everyone was there to welcome them back and find out about the vacation. Muriel told them about her articles and the meeting with Mary. Julie updated them on her progress at the café.

"We are officially opening next Saturday at 6 am," said Julie. "Everyone's welcome to their first coffee. I'm excited but terrified at the same time."

"You'll do great," said Muriel. "We are picking up the new cook tomorrow morning, which will give her some time to get organized."

"You found someone?" asked Elizabeth.

"Yes, it was a recommendation from François, your partner. A woman he knows who needs a fresh start," explained Julie. "We talked and she will be a good fit, I also hired a dishwasher."

"Oh, I almost forgot Dad," said Julie. "J.R. wrote to say he might be promoted and transferred to the base in Ottawa. It's closer than Trenton and he would be able to see you more often."

John Ross, or J.R. was Harry's son and Julie's half-brother. He was in the Air Force as a mechanic and between travel and moves to different bases Harry never saw him enough. It had been a shock for him to find out he had a sister, but their bond had been immediate.

Peter told Elizabeth all was well in the office, all the reports were done, and a few new cases had come in.

"You should go away more often," said Grandfather John. "I had a wonderful time, kids in and out, full table for dinners, lots to do. Harry might be too old for me to hang around with!"

They moved to the living room for coffee and Harry played a few pieces on the piano. It was a nice ending to the vacation. When it was time for Elizabeth to go back to her apartment, she didn't expect to feel so torn about it. Happiness was growing on her and she found it quite addictive.

"Everyone, before you go, next Friday I'm doing dinner for Elizabeth's birthday," said Harry. "The birthday is mid-week, but Friday seems a good time to get everyone together. Once the café opens some of you will want early nights.

They all agreed to meet again on Friday. Muriel and Elizabeth walked down the lane to her apartment.

"You know the book you loaned me," said Elizabeth. "How did you get it?"

"Did you enjoy it? I bought it in Ottawa," said Muriel.

Elizabeth had a sigh of relief until Muriel said, "I didn't realize you had ordered a copy for yourself; it came in while you were gone."

Elizabeth knew the vacation was over.

Chapter 5

The next morning Elizabeth was up early and glad that Muriel had stocked up on bread and coffee. Her apartment was conveniently located at the back of the property she owned. There was a hardware store tenant on the ground floor and two offices on the second floor. One of them was *Grant & Lefebvre Private Investigators*. She let Muriel sleep in and walked over to the office with her second cup of coffee.

Peter had not arrived yet, but he had piled the incoming mail on her desk. Elizabeth noticed the parcel Muriel had mentioned, the book from J.S. Simmons. She sorted the mail, mostly looking for a letter from Edward Rushton.

Edward had written back, concerned over her comments. He said he had people looking into the book and any connections to either Josephine Smith or work Elizabeth's husband had been doing at the time of his death. Edward suggested a phone call once she was back at work. Her next move was to look at the parcel itself. It was a book that had come directly from the publisher, but she never ordered it. There was a handwritten note inside that said, *Now is the time.* She would have to look at the other note she had from Josephine Smith to see if the writing was hers.

Elizabeth was feeling burdened by all this, yet again. She had thought that all was behind her. Now circumstances and revelations were throwing her back into the ring with Josephine Smith in the shadows.

Peter walked in, juggling the door, a coffee and the day's paper. He had changed so much since she had hired him. Her nephew had been a student all of nineteen years old, fresh-faced and naïve. Now he was living on his own, had a car, and had learned much about the world from his personal experiences and work at the agency. These days he spent a lot of time with Julie, Harry's daughter, claiming friendship only. Elizabeth had some doubts about that, but she would not pry. Peter had met Julie before anyone even knew she was related to Harry. Peter loved Elizabeth dearly, he respected her and looked out for her. They had a good relationship and he often confided in her but had not said much about Julie.

She quickly brought him up to date on the book, the possible link to Josephine Smith and her reach to Edward Rushton. Peter knew all the cast of characters, having been involved in the peculiar case that had put both his and Elizabeth's life in danger. She also told him about the manuscript she had received at the end of the case.

"So, you didn't read it?" asked Peter. "If it was me, I would have been too curious to leave it."

"By the time the dust settled, I was only looking to forget about the whole thing," replied Elizabeth. "I wasn't even sure what had happened to her after she left Canada. I'd assumed she would hunker down and retire. Not write a novel, a best-seller to boot, about international affairs and spying."

That train of thought was interrupted by the ring of the phone. It was Edward Rushton, who was quick to jump to the point.

"Hi, Elizabeth. I expect you had a wonderful time away," he said. "Interesting turn of events with the *Spies and Innuendos* novel from our Josephine Smith."

"Hi, Edward. Are you thinking it's her? If it is, what is she doing?" asked Elizabeth. "Did you see any possible links to William's crash?"

"We are still looking into that," he said. "Do you remember when you sold the house? What did you do with the things that were in William's office? Any paperwork? Did he have a safe at home?"

"I put everything in boxes and then in Margie's basement," she replied. "I never went through it. I imagined I was going to sort it later but I never got around to it."

"Can you get that stuff back and have a look through it?" asked Edward. "I will send you anything I have here. Security clearances, of course, and with that you are back on the payroll of the Department of Justice."

"Ok, I will let you know what I have. And thanks Edward, I'm sorry to drag you into something like this again."

"No worries, I'll pull Santini back into it as well. Might as well get the RCMP up to scratch early. Take care and talk to you soon," ended Edward.

"Peter, how do you fancy a trip to your cousin Margie in Ottawa?" asked Elizabeth. "I will call her; I need you to bring back some boxes from her house. Things from William's office."

"Sure. I can bring my little sister along for company. She might enjoy a visit with the baby and the twins."

"And Peter, Muriel and Margie have no idea why I'm looking into this, so please don't tell them anything until we know more."

This was going to be difficult. She would need to talk to Harry, the poor man would worry again. If it involved William's death, she would have to tread carefully with Muriel staying with her now. She would not be detached from any conversation about this investigation. Margie would also find out.

She phoned Margie, letting her know that Peter would drop by to pick up the boxes. She said she only needed to sort through some of the paperwork but did not let on any further.

At 10 am Julie picked up Muriel and they headed to the north end train station to pick up Marianne, the café's new cook. The train from Montreal had been a touch early and when they pulled up a young woman was waiting for them. Julie knew she would be in her early thirties but she looked younger. The lonely figure, with her small suitcase, tentatively smiled at them. She had thick brown hair in a fashionable cut and grey eyes that betrayed a touch of weariness.

"Hi, you must be Marianne," said Julie. She introduced Muriel and they headed to the café on Second Street.

Marianne seemed a bit shy and unsure, but when she walked into the coffee shoppe, she was pleased.

"Thank you very much, for doing this," she said with a slight French accent. "I am grateful for the opportunity."

All three sat down at a table with fresh coffee and a few pastries. Marianne was curious about the business and her role in it.

"The size is good, and it feels so fresh and new," she said. "When I was young, back home in Quebec, I worked in a lumber camp over the winters. I fed hungry lumberjacks three meals a day. This will be a breeze, mind you it's been a while but my heart will be into this."

"And working for a woman will be so nice," she added. "François mentioned that I needed to get away, didn't he? He has been so nice to me; he is one of the good ones."

"He didn't go into details, but if this works for both of us, I'm happy," said Julie.

"I'm not hiding or in any trouble with the law," Marianne reassured her. "It's a long time ago now, but I met a man while I was at the lumber camp. Come spring I followed him to Montreal to find out he already had a wife and family. I ended up at the train station with no money and nowhere to go. I met a woman who said she could help me with work, but that ended up being the red-light district in downtown Montreal."

"I'm so sorry," said Julie. "I was in foster care and I know how it can turn out."

"Yes, I saw many girls come and go," said Marianne. "Last year I said I didn't want to work that way anymore. It didn't go over well with the boss and that landed me in the hospital. François who had kept his connections, learned about it. He made sure I wouldn't be bothered anymore and suggested I come here."

"We found you a room down the road, so you can walk to work and be right downtown," said Muriel.

"Are you all right with money?" asked Julie. "Do you need an advance?"

"No, I'm good. François gave me a small loan to start."

"Ok. We will take you to your room and tomorrow we can start looking at the menu and the setup. We open this coming Saturday, so that gives us a few days to try things out and see if anything is missing. I also hired a young man, Paul Laurin. He will be our dishwasher and general help. We also have to figure out days off."

Julie had booked a room for her at Jarvo's Boarding House, 40 First Street East, right beside St Paul's United Church. It was close to work through the laneway as they showed Marianne on their way there. The room was small but comfortable and the atmosphere was homey. Mrs. Jarvo was happy to have a new boarder and explained all the house rules.

"You can move later on if you want something different," said Julie. "Cornwall has a large francophone population and I'm sure you can make a home here. For meals, you can take breakfast and lunch at the coffee shoppe, so there is only dinner to take care of."

"Oh, thank you, this is so nice," said Marianne. "A room of my own, safe and private."

"We'll leave you to unpack and explore around if you want. The street over to your left has lots of shops if you need anything. We will see you tomorrow."

Julie thanked Muriel for the drive to the train station. "I was glad to do it," said Muriel. "She is going to work out well, I think. You know you should ask Peter or your father to show you how to drive. It's one more way to independence, as I see it."

"Who do you think would have more patience? Dad or Peter?" asked Julie.

"Definitely Harry," said Muriel as they both laughed.

Chapter 6

Elizabeth knew that Harry had no plans for the evening, so she walked over after dinner. As she walked up, she could hear the piano. John came to the door and welcomed her in.

"Miss me already?" asked Harry. But as he walked over, he could see the worry on her face.

"More news from Josephine Smith I gather. Dad made coffee or do you prefer something stronger?"

"Coffee will be fine," she said, walking over to the sofa. "I need a clear head."

John brought in a tray and asked whether they wanted to be alone to talk but Elizabeth didn't mind if he stayed. He was a clear thinker and his presence always comforting. Elizabeth told them of her conversation with Edward and where they were at with the investigation. She stressed that this had broader implications for the whole family.

Harry understood that too well. Earlier this year, he had faced the return of his wife and her violent death. He had wanted, as much as possible to lessen the pain it caused his son J.R. and his newly found sister.

"One thing for certain," said John, "you need to find out if it was an accident. If it wasn't then you need to find out who's responsible."

"Do you have some sort of report on the crash itself? Anything about the car? I could look and see if I can spot anything suspicious," asked Harry. "You said he drove a Studebaker?"

"Yes, 1929 Studebaker Commander," answered Elizabeth. "He lost control on a country road and the car went off the road, hitting a tree."

"So, you would think, steering or brakes, to go off the road," said John.

"Could have been a hit and run," said Harry. Another car could have hit him, or he could have tried to avoid being hit and steered off the road. If it was on a quiet side road, there's not a lot of traffic to see it happen or help. As for sabotage causing a mechanical break, a Commander had a simple Bendix mechanical brake system. Weakening the links could have caused a malfunction but it would be difficult to predict when the breaks would let go. To me, another car forcing him off the road at the right moment would be more successful."

Elizabeth gasped and Harry took her hand, "I'm sorry, Liz. I didn't mean to be so graphic."

"No, it's ok, it needs to be said," said Elizabeth. "Once I get the paperwork from Edward, I will show it to you. Nobody suspected foul play at the time so they might not have been so thorough."

John cleared up the coffee and left them alone

for a while. When Elizabeth first met Harry, she imagined her head would fit nicely on his shoulder. She liked that he wasn't thin, but rather softly padded to be comfortable when leaning on him. And he always smelled so nice. She made the most out of that now.

"I will have to bring Muriel up to speed on all this," she said. "You know her now and that won't be easy or quiet, but I can't hide things from her."

"I know," said Harry. "She is always welcome here if she needs to talk. Grandpa John has taken a fancy to her and he is a good listener."

She said goodbye at the door and promised to call tomorrow.

Peter came back from Ottawa with six large boxes marked "Office." Elizabeth didn't have the heart to start going through them just yet. She was waiting for a confirmation from Edward that William's work might have led to someone doing him harm. All was good in her world right now; tonight was her birthday dinner and she was looking forward to it. Her friend Mary could not make the dinner but she said she would drop by for coffee and cake. Elizabeth was hoping there was cake, Harry had done the planning and she didn't know a thing about it.

She opted to wear a flowery summer dress, something like what she wore the first time she met Harry when she bought a car from him. Muriel and Peter had already gone over there. When she entered the foyer, everyone yelled "Happy Birthday" and she was surprised to see Margie and James. They didn't have the grandkids in tow.

"Happy Birthday, Mother," said Margie. "James' mother is babysitting the whole weekend, so we decided to come down. We are staying at the Cornwallis Hotel."

"Tomorrow morning, we are SLEEPING in!" said James. "My mother was eager to spend some time with her new grandson and we were happy to oblige. I love the little guy to pieces but between the twins and him, there's not a minute left."

"I'm glad you could come," said Elizabeth. "I'll be taking the girls with me once school is over, I miss them."

John was in his element as the house was full of young people and he was happy serving drinks and teasing everyone. Elizabeth kissed Harry and thanked him for arranging all this. Julie suggested he play a few songs on the piano while they waited for dinner. He was happy to play for them.

Mrs. Denny had volunteered to stay until the start of the meal. She had outdone herself, with Elizabeth's favourite dish of lasagna and toasted fresh bread. She said she wanted to do garlic bread but Mr. Warner had vetoed that idea! And of course, there was cake and candles fortunately not the exact number of fifty-one. Elizabeth made her wish and blew them out. Just in time Mary walked in and was introduced to those she didn't know yet.

"Now, it's time for the birthday gift," said Harry. "I wondered what would be special enough and something came to me when I was thinking of my mother."

Everyone was curious as Harry brought in a large

square wrapped in brown paper. "I apologize in advance for the choice of wrapping, but I couldn't find a mix of decorative and sturdy."

Elizabeth ripped the paper and found a large quilt. She unfolded it on the sofa. It was magnificent. The border was cream with a string of little blue flowers, another similar border with smaller flowers and then a white border. The centre pieces, all squares, were of alternating white and blue flowers. In the centre four of the squares were different.

Harry explained, "My sister made this with the Moulinette quilting guild from the St. Andrews United Church. The four squares in the middle represent things that are special to us. A book for the first case, a hat like Sherlock Holmes for the detective that Elizabeth is, a cat for Dusty, which I gave you, and finally a small car. Because that's how we met."

Harry turned around to see how they liked it and saw that all the women had tears in their eyes. "Is the little car too much?" he asked, unsure whether this gift was a success or not.

Elizabeth hugged him. "Oh Harry, this is so sweet," she said. He made a sigh of relief.

"Well, Harry, man, you raised the bar so high with this one, there is no way any of us men can ever measure up," said James.

"How did you come up with this idea?" asked John.

"We went to your house, on the farm and I looked in on your bedroom. I remembered Mother always having a quilt on the bed. And she had told me that all quilts have stories attached to them. They are often personal gifts or made with scraps of fabric that have meaning to a family," said Harry.

Mary walked by Elizabeth and said in her ear, "See, I told you he was a good one."

"Drinks anyone?" asked John. "Tomorrow everyone's going to Julie's new restaurant for breakfast."

"I'm sending all the guys for a coffee break, better be ready," said Harry.

John suggested to Harry that he take Elizabeth home as she needed help carrying the quilt. He hinted that it was heavy and the young people were not ready to go home for a while. Elizabeth agreed and they took their leave.

The next morning, they all made their way to *The Cornwall Coffee Shoppe* for its grand opening. Julie was already taking orders, Marianne was on the grill, and Paul clearing up. Peter had volunteered for preparation and coffee support.

When Harry and Elizabeth came in, they managed to get a table from a couple just leaving. Julie came over for their order, out of breath but glowing.

"This is crazy, Dad. It's been nonstop since the door opened at 6 am! But we're holding our own. Grandfather was already here with his friend Ruby." Elizabeth had met Mrs. Ruby Eastman on a train voyage to Philadelphia. They had hit it off and when Ruby came back to Cornwall, Elizabeth introduced her to John.

"I told everyone I knew to show up, I guess the publicity worked," Harry said with pride.

They ordered toast and coffee. By the time lunch was ready to roll out, Margie and James came in and took over their table. The lineup never stopped. Harry and Elizabeth decided to pitch in. Elizabeth and Muriel grabbed an apron and moved in so that Marianne and Peter could take a break. Harry took a pad and went out for orders. By the time 2 p.m. rolled around and the place was finally empty, Peter ran to the door to lock it.

"That's it, I'm done," he said. "And we're closed tomorrow!"

Everyone came back to sit and relax and laugh about their day.

"Mr. Warner," said Marianne. "Don't take this the wrong way, but you must work on your handwriting. Some of those orders were hard to figure out. I couldn't decide if they ordered toast or roast!"

Chapter 7

On Monday morning, came the news she didn't want to hear. Edward phoned her to say William had been working on a Russian spy infiltration into Canada, shortly before his accident. He had also been in touch, once again with Josephine Smith.

"Thanks, Edward," said Elizabeth. "What's the next step?"

"Has Josephine been in contact with you since you received the book?" he asked.

"No but I will let you know if she does," said Elizabeth. "There has to be more to this, why did she reach out, what does she want and why now?"

"All good questions. Let's work on the accident and wait for her to make a move," said Edward. "Keep me in the loop. I talked with Santini; he says hello by the way. You have an admirer there."

"You know, every time I see him, I want to tickle him to see if he can laugh," said Elizabeth. Santini was not what she would call an open book.

"Yes, he is a man of very few words. Best poker face ever," said Edward. "Take care."

Elizabeth asked Peter to bring the boxes out of storage and into her apartment. He was ready to leave when they heard heavy footsteps on the stairs and a series of curse words that would make a hardened sailor blush. It was Muriel, at her best.

"Wow, watch your language," said Elizabeth. "Where did you learn to talk like that?"

"College," Muriel said.

"That was my money well spent, I can see," said her mother.

"They turned down my article," Muriel said as she shook the coat tree. "They liked my piece on the anniversary of the town, but they won't publish my piece on the housing crisis too depressing they said. I'm fuming."

"Yes, we noticed. But that's not necessarily the end of it. The work is good, we can use it differently," said Elizabeth. "We can talk to Mary about it and see what she thinks."

"Good idea, I will call her," said Muriel.

"I want you and Peter at my apartment tonight, I need your help going over some of your father's paperwork. I will tell you what it's about."

"Sure, see you at dinner. I'm going to see Mary Randolph," said Muriel as she walked out.

"Ok, Peter, I guess the storm has blown over. You can get those boxes in and are you good to come over tonight?" asked Elizabeth.

"Absolutely, Aunt Liz, I know it's important."

Pitt Street was a hive of activity and the sun

shone through the windows. A short escape was in order, some fresh air and a walk would do wonders for her headache. She would also pick up a few snacks for the evening, not that she needed to fuel Muriel's hyperactivity any further.

There was mail for her and a flimsy air mail envelope from France stood out. There was also a note to drop by the counter.

"Mrs. Grant, we have received something and it might be for you," said the postal worker. "It's strange but it is addressed to the hardware store in your building but to Elizabeth Richards. It was returned from the store because they don't have anyone by that name. "I thought you might know."

"Yes, it is strange, but Richards is my maiden name," said Elizabeth. The postal worker gave her a large envelope with an airmail sticker, from France."

Elizabeth reflected on the last case she worked on involving Josephine Smith. There, she had managed to move a rare book from Canada to the US mixing names and addresses. There was a sense of déjà vu here. This much attention from someone who had tried to kill her could not be good news. Unless Josephine Smith hoped she could make amends by sending a birthday card.

Back in the office, she threw the two letters on her desk. She would need a clear head to deal with this and she had other things to worry about. She knew the evening would be difficult.

The phone rang and it was Muriel. She was with Mary and they wondered whether she would like to join them for coffee. Elizabeth agreed to meet them at Julie's coffee shoppe. Mary had not been there yet and Elizabeth would do anything to get her mind off the bigger things she had to deal with.

"Busy place," said Mary. "I certainly like the décor with all those old photos!"

"That was Mother's idea," said Muriel. "The place is doing well. Julie is happy."

They had coffee in front of them and Muriel added a large piece of carrot cake. "I love this, it pays to know the owner," said Muriel.

"So, the newspaper will not print your article?" asked Mary. "It's too bad because it's well written and certainly does express our concerns."

"It doesn't mean it has to be the end of it though," said Elizabeth. "The housing situation and the welfare of some in the community is a growing concern."

"Perhaps, there is another way," said Mary. "To gather support, but less publicity. Let's work with influential individuals instead."

"What are you thinking about?" asked Muriel."

"We could still use what you have written but disseminate the information to a few people, like aldermen and businessmen who would support our efforts," Mary suggested.

"Good idea," said Elizabeth. "Harry, as a businessman and part of the Kinsmen Club could help with this. The Kinsmen know firsthand some of the issues, and so will others. If we get backing and bring a proposal to City Hall, they might do something."

"It is a reality that in order to move this along we need men to champion it," said Mary.

Muriel, who had perked up, was happy with where this was going. "So, what's next?"

"Let's make copies of your article, and I can send them to those who can help us," said Mary. "We can have a meeting and look at a strategy, perhaps ask to present something at a city council meeting."

"Great idea," said Muriel. "I'm going back to Ottawa in a few days, back to work, but I might ask for some vacation time. I might be needed here for other things…"

"Is everything alright Elizabeth?" asked Mary. "You are far away in your thoughts."

"I'm sorry, things have come up," said Elizabeth. "Remember last year, that Josephine Smith investigation, well she's back for more. She's made some insinuations and I'm involved with Ottawa again."

"Oh, not good news," said Mary. "I'm here to listen and help, as always."

"Thanks, I'm going back to the office now and I might call you later," said Elizabeth. She knew well that her friendship with Mary was important in times like these.

Muriel and Mary stayed at the café for a while longer, discussing copies to be made and potential recipients of the letters and articles.

Elizabeth was dragging her feet about getting back to work. Instead, she decided to phone Laura, Harry's sister, and thank her for making the quilt she received for her birthday. She had wanted to go to Moulinette and thank the quilters in person, but she wasn't sure what day they met. She opted for a phone call instead.

"Hi Laura, I hope I'm not disturbing you, but I wanted to thank you for the Quilt," said Elizabeth. "It's absolutely lovely."

"Thank you," said Laura. "You know it's funny but I never thought my brother would come up with such an idea for a gift, all on his own! From what I know, he'd be more likely to give you a set of wipers for your car!"

"It was so sweet of him, we had tears in our eyes," said Elizabeth. "The workmanship is so fine, and the colours are all my favourites."

"I'm glad you like it," said Laura. "The quilters from our group enjoyed working on it."

"What day do you meet? I'd like to thank all of them in person," said Elizabeth.

"We quilt on Wednesday evening," said Laura. "Everyone would love to meet you and see who merited such a gift."

Chapter 8

The only one that was looking forward to an evening of rummaging through William's paperwork was Dusty the cat. He was the grey tabby that Harry had found in the remains of the fire on Pitt Street last year. He had given it to Peter with a message to bring the cat to Elizabeth for safekeeping. She had protested for a couple of minutes but couldn't resist the soot-covered fur ball. The choice of name had been self-evident. Peter played matchmaker by supplying Harry with news of the kitten, hoping it would be an opener to further conversations between him and his aunt. The rest is history as they say.

Dusty was intrigued by the boxes, and the piles of paperwork, claiming his territory in the middle of it all. He tried to lay down as large as he could on every piece of paper on the floor. Muriel and Peter were sitting in Elizabeth's small living room, waiting for directions on how to proceed.

"These are the boxes from William's home office," said Elizabeth. "We are looking for anything around the time of his death, so spring 1930. What he might have been working on, any appointments, notes and the likes. I don't expect much, because I don't think he brought any confidential material home, but let's find out."

"Did you go through this at the time?" asked Muriel.

"No, I thought I would do it later," explained Elizabeth. She gave Muriel a glass of wine and a small Scotch for herself and Peter. It was a taste she had acquired from her husband and had passed on to Peter.

Each took a box and sorted through the findings. "I have a box on the side if we are throwing away anything and another one for you Muriel if you want to keep something for yourself or Margie," said Elizabeth.

It was unmistakeably sombre and sad, going back so many years, remembering how things were. William didn't work much at home. He preferred to spend time with his girls, as he liked to say. Most of the paperwork was copies of bills, bank statements, family photos and one of a much younger Elizabeth.

Muriel reached into another box and pulled out some coloured pieces of paper. "Look, Mother, a bunch of my drawings when I was six years old!" Muriel put those in her box to keep and wiped her eyes before moving on.

"If there is anything about Josephine Smith, let me know," said Elizabeth. "Edward Rushton said that William had contacted her again."

"Do we know where he was going on the day of the crash?" asked Peter.

"No, it was a workday, so we thought he was

possibly on his way to a meeting," explained Elizabeth.

"What day was the accident again?" he asked working his way through an agenda book.

"March 12th, I think it was a Wednesday," said Elizabeth.

"I have something here in the day planner, March 12th, a name, Sam Carr. That's the only appointment for the day."

"Ok, I will take this down and send it to Rushton," said Elizabeth.

"There is another file, looks like background notes, for a Kathleen Willsher, coming to work as a secretary at the British High Commission in Ottawa," said Peter.

"One more for Rushton. He is also sending us some files relating to the accident to look at," said Elizabeth.

"So, we know that Josephine Smith is J.S. Simmons, the author of that spy bestseller," said Peter.

Muriel immediately looked up with a puzzled look on her face. Elizabeth thought this might be a suitable time to tell her more, so she explained her encounters with Josephine Smith, from 1903 to last year, and told her about the manuscript in her safe. It didn't take long for Muriel to link one thing to the other.

"The novel, the one I loaned you, some part of it had to do with Father's accident!" exclaimed Muriel as she grew angrier. "That chapter about a lawyer working for his country, and killed in an automobile accident was Dad????"

"It might be, Muriel, that's what we are trying to figure out," said Elizabeth almost apologizing for the hurt.

Knowing her daughter, Elizabeth was expecting full-blown rage, but Peter went to sit beside Muriel and put his arm around her. She melted into his shoulders and sobbed. Elizabeth picked up the glasses and went into the kitchen, she also had to steady herself.

When she went back to the living room, everyone decided to call it a night. The phone rang and Elizabeth knew it was Harry, but she didn't pick it up. She was still knee-deep in the past and couldn't reconcile it with the present.

Chapter 9

Elizabeth's day in the office started with a headache due to the lack of sleep and the nightmares she had when she was finally able to doze off. The sadness she had felt last night had made way for an all-out anger. She was angry at Josephine Smith for messing up with her life again. Was this her plan for revenge? How dare she write about her husband's death in a spy novel! He had been a good man, he loved her and their daughters, and he was real to them, not a character in a dime store novel! She held *Spies and Innuendos* in her hand and threw it across the room.

The flying hardcover missed François Lefebvre by inches as he walked into the room. Elizabeth stood up and he saw how miserable she looked and reached out for her. She was one of the strongest women he knew and she didn't fall apart easily. She shed a few tears on the lapel of his expensive, tailor-made jacket.

Muriel and Harry walked in as she pulled away and apologized. There was a brief awkward silence broken by Peter, walking in and asking, "Coffee anyone?"

"The office is getting crowded, the only one missing is the cat," said Elizabeth. They each stumbled into a reason to be there.

"Peter called me," said François. "Seems you might need a bit of help looking into things."

"You didn't answer my call last night, so I hoped things weren't too hard for you, so I came over," said Harry.

"I live here," said Muriel.

"Enough," said Elizabeth now back into her private investigator mode.

"Peter knows we need to investigate Carr, so François can help with that and a link with Kathleen Willsher. Muriel can finish with the boxes in the living room, and Harry is taking me for breakfast," directed Elizabeth.

"Yes boss!" said Peter. He had a feeling Elizabeth was back and angry. Watch out Josephine Smith!

Elizabeth grabbed a file from her desk and pushed Harry out the door.

They walked over to Julie's coffee shoppe, Harry finding out how things had gone the night before. They sat at a table in the back.

"It's ok Harry, you can say that I look terrible. I won't be offended," she smiled.

"You're always beautiful to me, my dear," replied Harry. "Did you eat anything? You should eat."

"Yes, I see comfort in scrambled eggs, bacon and warm buttered toast," said Elizabeth.

Julie came over to take their orders, she was

happy and smiling but frowned when she looked at Elizabeth and asked how she was doing. Elizabeth trusted Peter not to leak information, but Julie didn't need a crystal ball to see that things were difficult.

"I have this for you," said Elizabeth as she pushed the folder towards Harry. "It's from the collision, photos and the various reports. I don't want to look at it, but maybe you'll spot something they haven't. I appreciate it."

He put the file aside and made room for the plates. He ate heartily but Elizabeth pushed her food around only taking a few bites.

"Did you find any leads in the boxes?" asked Harry.

"Yes, I need to contact Edward Rushton to give him some names and dates and see where it goes," said Elizabeth. "I also received two letters from Josephine Smith, I haven't opened them yet. That's my next project."

"Didn't you say that your husband was working on Russian involvement in Canada?" asked Harry. "That's how she could be involved, having been a spy of sorts."

"Yes, but I'm wondering why she is reaching out now…" she said. "And what does she want me to do with the manuscript I have in my safe? When she sent a note saying, 'Now is the time' what does it mean? Time to release her memoirs? To whom, the government, the press?"

"I think you need to walk through this step by step," suggested Harry. "Let Peter and François help and see where it leads."

"Always the calming influence, you are," said Elizabeth. "Do you know where I would like to be right now?"

"Four years back before any of this happened," said Harry sadly.

"No, none of us can go back, and feeling sorry wouldn't change anything, I can't get lost in the past. I was happy there, but there is also my happiness in the present and hopefully the future," she smiled.

"Remember the cottage on the lake while we were on vacation?" asked Elizabeth. "I would like to be back on the lake, in the boat taking in the sunset on the mirrored lake."

"We could do something like that after you put Josephine Smith back in her place. You won't have peace before you do that," said Harry.

"Liz, do you like François?" He was thinking back on the scene when he walked into the office.

"Harry Warner! Be serious, I needed an expensive suit to cry on and he was handy."

"As for Sam Carr," said Peter. "We need to find out where he lived at the time. Was it anywhere near where Uncle William had his accident?"

"We need to figure out if the accident happened on the way there or after their meeting if they did meet," said François. "Santini from the RCMP could also tell us if Carr was known to them, or under investigation. We could figure out why William wanted to meet with him."

"I'll phone Santini and you can flip through the stuff Rushton sent yesterday," said François. "Do you want to do lunch at Julie's after? I would like to see how Marianne is doing."

"Good idea, I'll grab Muriel, she's always starving," said Peter. "And Marianne is doing well, she looks happy with the work and the move."

Elizabeth came back as they were all heading out to lunch. She sat at her desk and decided to open the two air mail letters she received from Saint-Lunaire, the resort town in France. The first larger envelope was, in fact, a birthday card. Elizabeth stopped wondering how Josephine knew her address, her maiden name and her birthday, it was a moot point in the whole saga. Purple flowers and ribbons encircled a *Bonne Fête*, with a smell of roses coming from the card. Elizabeth thought it looked like something you would give an ageing grandmother, quickly realizing that it was exactly what she was. Inside was this cryptic writing:

Many happy returns my dear,

If being 51 is like being 6,

A to be 6 again!

Was Josephine saying she was going senile? It was signed simply J. Then on the inside cover a Shakespeare poem:

All the world's a stage,

And all the men and women merely players;

They have their exits and their entrances;

And one man in his time plays many parts,

His acts being seven ages.

And then the lover,
Sighing like furnace, with a woeful ballad
Made to his mistress' eyebrow.

Then a soldier,
Full of strange oaths, and bearded like the pard,
Jealous in honour, sudden and quick in quarrel,
Seeking the bubble reputation
Even in the cannon's mouth.

Elizabeth remembered her short meeting with Josephine Smith, on the train to Philadelphia, last year. She had been a mysterious woman, with good looks and a cunning theatrical demeanour, which gave away little of the true woman. But she had been a successful spy most of her life, so perhaps she got lost in the role.

Elizabeth opened the second smaller envelope, a few thin sheets of that light airmail paper. She didn't know what to make of that one. No date, no header, just confusing text.

YGS IGXX ATOUTY XAYYG

Elizabeth realized she needed another coffee.

Chapter 10

Marianne was happy to see François again and jumped into his arms when he came by the kitchen. Peter and Muriel took a table, and wondered at the scene, what the relationship between François and Marianne had been. François came back to sit with them and tried to clean something off his lapel.

"Good day for you, but tough on the jacket, hey…tears and grease," commented Muriel.

François realized she was including the scene with her mother this morning and decided to play along. "Small price to pay when supporting beautiful women."

Muriel smiled, looked for the special of the day and claimed she was starving.

"Julie and Marianne are getting along famously," said Peter. "People enjoy her cooking and she is fast."

"She said she loves the town and is making friends," said François. "The only adjustments were getting used to the early hours and the day shift was a change for her. But her health is better for it, I see that. She is starting to make plans, I'm happy for her."

They ate quickly and told Muriel to go back to the office on her own as François and Peter wanted to drop in and see Harry before going back.

Harry was in his office and closed the door behind them as he offered them seats. He opened a folder on his desk and showed them the photos of the car and the reports.

"So, it was a quiet country road, along farmland, a few trees along the fence line on the gravel road. He was heading east, back towards Metcalfe Road and then north to Ottawa probably," said Harry.

"We are looking into that," said Peter. "We think he went to see someone named Sam Carr."

"So, the funny thing is, if you look at the photos, it doesn't seem like he was speeding, and there is no sign of emergency braking," said Harry. "It's almost as if the car glided off the road to rest against the tree."

"Yes, I see that," said François. "And he was driving a big car. There doesn't appear to be a lot of damage."

"A Studebaker Commander, with a long front end," said Harry. "And that's the thing if he would have hit the tree with any speed it would show. Of course, there was an impact so his head and chest would have hit the steering wheel hard. But enough to die from it? I have to wonder."

"Does the report show anything wrong mechanically?" asked Peter.

"Not really," replied Harry. "The way it looks, I

don't think they suspected foul play."

"Does the file contain anything on William's body?" asked François. "A check for booze, drugs, health issues?"

"I don't see it in this file, perhaps his office has that. What are you thinking?" asked Harry. "A heart attack?"

"No, well, perhaps," said François. "But given that we might be looking at murder, to stop him from talking about things he found out, anything is possible."

"Could Carr have given him drugs? Poison?" asked Peter.

"I don't know but they would have had to be sure it would kill him; they couldn't rely on a crash to do the trick. If he felt unwell, he could have stopped on the side of the road," said François. "Thank you, Harry, for your opinion on this, much appreciated. What do you want us to say to Elizabeth?"

"Maybe you should mention what you suspect first, as it is part of your investigation," said Harry. "I'll be there for her if she needs me."

Elizabeth went for a breath of fresh air, first walking down to the canal to see the ships pass through town. A few of the sailors waved at her as she went by, and that made her smile. She cut across Central Park. The park had a large fountain in the centre, with pathways leading to it, there was a big bandshell with two cannons from the 1890s. A pool for the children had been built a few years back. She sat on a bench looking at the children running around the fountain and she realized how much she missed her grandchildren. She noticed Marianne, the cook from Julie's Coffee Shoppe, and waved at her. She must have just finished her shift. She came to sit with her, looking up and enjoying the sun on her face.

"How are you settling in?" asked Elizabeth. "Is the room to your liking?" Marianne's boarding house was next to St Paul's United Church, which was beside the park.

"Mrs. Jarvo has been nice and I couldn't think of a better location," Marianne said. "Although there is something comical about a sinner like me living next to a Church…and a protestant one to boot. I hear them singing on Sunday morning, I think they sing more than we Catholics do. It's nice."

"Yes, they do, there are five churches within a few blocks around here and they all have choirs," said Elizabeth. "Wait until they all start having bake sales!"

"I'm so glad François suggested I come here," said Marianne. "I've stopped smoking, I'm out in the sunshine, and I'm proud of my work now. But I still think about the girls back on Clark Street, some were my friends."

"It must be difficult for you. I understand, but you deserve to make a go of it, for yourself," said Elizabeth.

"I plan to, I also wrote to my mother back in the Laurentians. It's a start," beamed Marianne.

Elizabeth noted that Marianne kept looking at the children playing around them. She ventured,

"Do you have children Marianne?"

"No, when you work in houses owned by Sonato, he has dirty doctors that look after that sort of thing," she said sadly. "The best girls, those who are regulars like judges and politicians, they can't afford to be out of service too long. We're like prize racehorses, aren't we?"

Marianne felt comfortable with Elizabeth and she continued, "I was pregnant before I came, that's why I wanted to get out of the game. But they didn't want to hear of it and I ended up in the hospital and I lost the baby."

"I'm so sorry," said Elizabeth. "Perhaps, later…"

"No, it's over for me," said Marianne.

Marianne got up and said she needed a few things from the shops on Pitt Street. Elizabeth walked with her stopping for the mail as Marianne continued to F. W. Woolworth.

The stack of mail included more files from Rushton. Those she would pass on to François and Peter. Aside from all the complications of this investigation, she was aware of the support she had now. When she opened the private investigation agency four years ago, it was only her and Peter. She was unsure of herself, of whether she could make a go of the business, or even if anyone would take her seriously. But now, she had achieved the credibility she had craved. It was a pleasant image for a moment at least.

Back in the office, Peter and François briefed her on their chat with Harry and discussed where they should look next. There was also a note from

Rushton saying he would be down on Monday to put everything together and tie up loose ends.

She told them she would work on the message from Josephine and have an early night. Muriel had another visit with Mary about their housing and community support project. She was going back to Ottawa on Sunday and planned to talk to Margie about their father.

In the evening Elizabeth called Mary, her best friend. She knew she could talk to her freely. She didn't need to guard herself as she did with Harry or Muriel. They both supported her but she didn't want to hurt either of them. She could share with Mary how hard it had been going over old times, and William's death again. There were twenty-seven years of history between them and she was angry it had been cut short. She wondered what their lives would have been like if they had been allowed to grow old together. But that didn't happen, and although she never stopped loving William, she couldn't think of her life now, without Harry. Mary would listen and understand.

Chapter 11

It was Saturday morning and both Elizabeth and François had decided to put in a few hours early in the day to sort things out. Elizabeth was surprised when Harry walked in, and he didn't look happy.

"Did you see Peter or Muriel, yet?" he asked.

"No, I don't think Peter is coming in and Muriel is still sleeping, she came in quite late last night," Elizabeth commented.

"I know. I had to bail them out of police custody," Harry said. "It seems they went out to celebrate at some east-end bar and a fight started."

"Peter?" asked Elizabeth. "It's not like him."

"No, actually it was Muriel," said Harry as François burst out laughing.

"Oh, give me a break, she's a grown woman, in a bar brawl?" she said.

"She called me, it seems she was less afraid of me than she was of you…," said Harry. "A couple of guys were bothering her and Julie and Peter got up to tell them to leave, but one of the guys went to hit Peter, and the other one was going for him, so Muriel hit him with a pool cue! Other people joined in; the police were called."

"I love coming to Cornwall," said François, still laughing, until Elizabeth shot him a glance that silenced him.

"I settled with the young men, so they wouldn't press charges, but I have to work on their car for free…so she owes me," says Harry.

On that comment, Peter walked in, grey-faced and tired… "You should have seen her, Aunt Liz, she was brilliant! Almost broke the pool cue over the guy's head!" he said.

"I'll have a talk with her as soon as she is up," said Elizabeth.

"Don't be too hard on her," said Harry. "I think all of her stress and anger needed an outlet; I don't think she'll be a repeat offender."

"We're barred from that place anyway," laughed Peter and he went over to François and did a couple of boxing jabs at him.

"Thank you, Harry, for going to get her," said Elizabeth. "I'll make sure she makes it up to you. Is she too old to be grounded?"

"I have to get back to work," he said. "I wanted to let you know."

"Rushton is coming down on Monday, a meeting to get everyone on the same page," said Elizabeth. "I'm wondering if we could meet at your place. If you wouldn't mind? The office is too small with all the paperwork and files."

"Sure, anytime," he replied. Elizabeth knew that by meeting at his place he would be included. She wondered if it would make him worry about her again.

Peter opted to stay for a while and pick up Julie after the restaurant closed.

"We found out that Sam Carr, lived off Metcalfe Road, around Leitrim. Given the time of day, it also makes sense that William was on his way back," said François.

"Do we know who called the police when it happened?" asked Peter as he searched through the paperwork. "It seems to have been a farmer out in his field, a Mr. Saunders."

"I wonder if he went to the car, or saw anything before the crash, another car or something?" asked Elizabeth.

"Perhaps it's worth asking, I don't see anything about an interview with him in the files," said François. "I might go for a drive on this lovely Saturday morning."

"I'll go with you," said Peter. "I will let Julie know. She wasn't impressed with the bar brawl either."

Elizabeth took out the two letters from Josephine Smith.

So obviously one must have something to do with the other. Cleverly they were sent to different names and different, albeit close, addresses. Individually each was meaningless. Looking at the two pieces of paper, she could deduce that it was numbers and letters.

If being 51 is like being 6,

A to be 6 again!

She took a pen and pad and played around, jotting down the alphabet to see if anything would jump out at her.

a b c d e f g h I j k l m n o p q r s t u v w x y z

51 and 6, so 5+1 = 6, then what?

A to be 6, was significant because one would normally write "Ah, to be 6 again!"

Did it mean that A would be 6? The sixth letter of the alphabet? So, from A she counted 6 down to get G. Based on this the word HOT would be N U Z. So, if you wanted to encrypt hot would write NUZ!

Elizabeth rewarded herself with a couple of Red Hots Cinnamon candies she kept on her desk. Onward we go! The numbers were in the birthday card with the poem, but she doubted the numbers applied to the prose, but to the second letter, the solitary grouping.

YGS IGXX ATOUTY XAYYOG

She would have to work it backwards so that Y would be six back for S, G replaced by A and S by M. The first word was SAM!!! The words were SAM CARR UNIONS RUSSIA!

That confirms it. They already knew Sam Carr had met with William and that he had been working on a spy infiltration before he passed away. "Unions" though was new to them. She would have to tell Rushton on Monday. Now it was time to go back to her apartment and have a chat with her daughter.

After lunch, she went for a walk, and to Eaton Groceteria looking for something for dinner. Going through the aisles she realized she needed quite a lot. Her shelves were bare, her mind hadn't been on domestic duties and although Muriel loved to eat, she never considered shopping. Dusty needed cat food, you can't live peacefully with a hungry cat, everyone knew that.

François and Peter came back late in the afternoon and told her about meeting with Mr. Saunders. He had seen the crash, the car sliding off the road and into the tree. He didn't see it speeding, there were no other cars around.

"He went to the car straight away, or rather as fast as he could driving an old tractor," said Peter. "But it was too late, he said. He went back to his house to call the police."

"It seemed to him though, that the police assumed it was straightforward," said François. "They didn't ask any questions."

Elizabeth sighed and told them about the word puzzles she solved. They agreed with her conclusions. A sheepish-looking Muriel wandered into the office, she smiled at Peter.

"Anyone for dinner?" Muriel asked. Elizabeth shook her head.

"I'm doing an early night, listening to the radio and that's it for me," said her mother.

"Pretty much the same here," said Peter. "No more walking on the wild side for me!"

"I'll take you for Chinese food if you want?" said François. "Elizabeth, I'll be on babysitting service, no bars, no pool cues, no worries."

Muriel thought it prudent, given the mood her mother was in, to keep silent and follow François out of the door.

They walked over to the New York Café, and looking over the menu, François noted that the Chinese options came with bread, butter and French fries. It was not something he was used to in Montreal's Chinatown. Muriel noticed that although he was not wearing a business suit his idea of casual was still classy and well-fitted.

"So, you like clothes?" asked Muriel. "Are your suits tailor-made, if I may be so bold?"

"Be so bold, my dear. After last night, it's a bit late to try and pretend you are shy and reserved," he smiled.

"I don't have a criminal record, in case you're curious…although there was that protest at Uni…never mind," said Muriel. "So, what about clothes?"

"Yes, I like to look good, and I know a tailor in Lachine," he said. "Am I vain? Maybe. I come from a large family…no money and lots of kids. I didn't have anything of my own, not even a pair of socks. It was hand-me-downs, either too big or too small. We got winter boots in the spring when richer people were donating them to charity. My parents did their best, but I noticed that people treated us differently."

"How so?" asked Muriel.

"Your clothes label you, or that's the way I saw it," he replied. "People take one look at you and know you're poor. So as soon as I made a bit of money, I got myself nicer clothes."

"You?" he asked. "I see you like the ladies' pants, and dresses only occasionally."

"Yes, it's the pockets you see," added Muriel. "Men are lucky, they get pockets, on shirts, pants, and jackets. You keep everything in your pockets. No such luck on women's wear, you get pockets on the odd apron, for handkerchiefs to wipe your kids' nose, and that's it.

"I see," said François. "I guess I never considered the challenge before."

"Oh, yes. Women need to dress for men, no bulging pockets with wallets and cigarette packs. Nothing to disrupt the flattering line. I go for wide-leg pants, I get pockets! A wife, girlfriends?" she asked.

"No wife, lots of girlfriends…" he smiled. "No that's not true, I would say girlfriends, less and less. Police work was not compatible with family life. I worked vice and it was long hours, difficult situations. Even with girlfriends, they soon get tired of cancelled dates. They want a fun guy. When they ask, "How was your day?" you see they don't really want to know."

He shook his head and moved on, "Boyfriends? If I may be so bold."

"No, nothing lasting," she replied. "I don't think men know how to take me, I'm a bit too independent, bad-tempered, career-oriented and I eat too much."

"Eat too much? I didn't know that was a criterion," he said. "I must be getting too old for the dating scene."

"Men like ladies with a light appetite. One who will always maintain that girlish figure, I tell you," said Muriel.

"Anything else I'm not current with?" he laughed.

"According to the 1930 dating guide I read, here are the pointers for women," she recites. "Don't sit in an awkward position, don't chew gum, don't look bored even if you are. Please and flatter your date by talking about things HE wants to talk about."

"I can see where you would find this challenging," teased François. She made a face at him, just before his chicken chow mein, duly accompanied by fries, arrived at their table.

"Do you have a crush on my mother?" she asked.

"I'm a bit old for crushes," he grinned. "But yes, I do, not in the way you imply though."

"It's professional only, I have a lot of respect for your mother," he explained. "She is strong and courageous; she forces me to do better. But I have seen her make crazy decisions too. It's a throwback from my policing days, you need to trust your partner. I know Elizabeth will always have my back."

"You have that right," said Muriel. "Dessert?"

"I'm a purist as far as Chinese food goes," he said. "I can tolerate adding French fries, but Chinese food and apple pie is a step too far for me. You go ahead. If you ever come to Montreal, I'll take you to

Chinatown, you'll see what I mean." Did he put out an invite? Good grief, get a grip, Lefebvre.

She obviously had no respect for the integrity of a proper Chinese meal, as she ordered chocolate cake. He only took coffee.

"You said you came from a large family?" asked Muriel.

"Yes, eleven kids," said François with some sadness in his eyes. "A good French Catholic family in east-end Montreal. The *curé* would line us up on his parish visits and give us *la bénédiction*... A blessing, thanking my parents for being such good Catholics."

"You wouldn't have a large family yourself?" asked Muriel.

"Absolutely not," he said firmly. "I can't remember my mother not being pregnant, or with a baby on her hip. She was thin, tired with dark lines under her eyes, she died young of consumption."

"Oh, I'm so sorry," she said. "Of course, birth control was difficult then…"

He looked at her with some surprise, he couldn't remember that subject coming up on a first date, any date. But this wasn't a date at all, he settled.

"Did I offend you? Too bold again?" asked Muriel. "See why I don't date!"

"Not at all, it's refreshing," he said. "No birth control but my father could have done better. He could have taken some care. The rich and educated Anglos up the hill had smaller families. They figured something out."

"This is another issue I care about," said Muriel.

"I volunteer at a clinic in Ottawa, for mothers and health care. I write information leaflets for them. To educate women but men also should be part of that conversation."

She apologized again and dug into the chocolate cake.

He smiled, "No, you're right. I worked vice and prostitution remember."

"Well, I'm full," she said.

"Give it half an hour," he teased.

On the corner of the placemat, she wrote down her phone number and gave it to him. "I'm going back to Ottawa tomorrow, but if something happens with the investigation you can let me know."

"Or if there is something wildly interesting that I could write about for the newspaper," she laughed.

"You're first on my list, should I ever feel the urge to speak with a journalist," he assured her. As he folded the paper, he noticed she had put a little heart instead of a dot over the i of Muriel. That was sweet he thought, and then the word idiot flashed in his mind again.

She wanted to go half on the dinner, but he wouldn't hear of it, he paid. He was old fashioned, or plain old as he reminded himself, limping slightly walking her back to Elizabeth's.

Muriel had gone back early on Sunday, with plans to drop by her sister. Their mother had mentioned the investigation to Margie but she thought it would be easier for the sisters to discuss it one on one. François opted to stay until Monday night to catch the briefing from Rushton.

Harry dropped in after dinner, the first time in a while that they didn't have everyone coming and going with no time for each other. Elizabeth made them tea and Harry sat at the kitchen table flipping through an old paper.

"Muriel stopped by before she went and thanked me for bailing her out," he said. "She will cover any expenses I have; grateful the guys didn't press charges."

"Thank you for doing that," Elizabeth said.

"You know, I was flattered that she thought about calling me first, she's normally so independent," he said.

"She trusted you; she needs good men in her life to tell her it's okay to be who she is," smiled Elizabeth. "It can be draining to go against the current."

"What are you doing, reading Dorothy Dix's advice column?" she noted.

"I was looking at the ads I put in for the garage and came across this advice on couples vacationing separately," he said.

Elizabeth looked over his shoulder at the column, one of the most popular in newspapers. Dorothy Dix didn't always give good advice but she still received hundreds of letters and the *Standard-Freeholder* published her regularly.

"She says that husbands and wives should have some sense about their vacations and each do what they want instead of sacrificing to the other," read Harry. "The time apart is the elixir of youth, a love potion that restores to them all the joys of the honeymoon."

"Sounds nice enough," says Elizabeth.

"Maybe but read this," said Harry, pointing to the next paragraph.

> *When they parted the man may have seen his wife only as a fat and fussy middle-aged woman and wondered what he saw in her…The woman may have beheld in her husband only a bay-windowed, bald-headed man casting her eyes wondering how he ever looked like a Fairy Prince…*

"Makes you wonder how long of a separate vacation that couple will need before getting back to the honeymoon phase!" laughed Harry.

"Thank God I'm not balding, but am I "bay-windowed," whatever that is?" he asked.

"No, you're a fine figure of a man, Harry Warner, and I'm still in the phase where I want to vacation with you, no worries there," she said, as she ruffled his bushy black hair.

Chapter 12

On Monday morning, Elizabeth had suggested they all meet at Harry's. He had a comfortable home next to his dealership on Second Street East. The foyer was central, with a living room on the right and a large dining room to the left. At the back was the kitchen where Mrs. Denny was waiting for them with coffee, tea and plates of sweets.

It looked like everyone had gathered for a board meeting. Edward Rushton, from the Department of Justice down from Ottawa at the head of the table, Elizabeth and Peter on one side, François and Harry on the other. Each had paperwork in front of them ready to make their contributions. John had opted to sit in the background but within hearing distance, of course.

"Thank you, Harry, for letting us meet here, I see much better cookies than anywhere else I could think of. Also, it goes without saying, but I'll say it anyway, that the two Mr. Warners will keep everything we say under strict confidentiality," said Rushton.

"I solemnly swear," said John in the back with a hand raised.

"Always the clown, hey Dad?" laughed Harry. "Sorry, Edward."

"I love it," says Rushton. "So, thanks to our Elizabeth here, we have you and the whole of the Federal Department of Justice, working overtime again."

"I would prefer if you put it on Josephine Smith's back, please," said Elizabeth.

"Yes, we thought she would enjoy her retirement a bit longer, but something brought her out again," said Rushton. "Either boredom or circumstance. The last person she met in England after last year's affair, was Sir Allan Stanfrey, a retired colonel, part of MI6, the British Foreign Service. Grapevine told us, she might have blackmailed him into providing a retirement income, relocation and a new name."

"Yes, I have been aware for a while now, that she is in Saint-Lunaire, in France. And her correspondence has been under J.S. Simmons," said Elizabeth.

"When you say, "Aware for a while" what do you mean exactly?" he said, eyes on Elizabeth.

"I have not been completely forthcoming, but last year she sent me some material with that contact information," said Elizabeth.

"Ok, I will stretch my trust in you to know what you were doing, but how far you can take this, we will see," said Rushton seriously. "She is letting you know via the book that there is something suspicious about William's death."

"Actually," says Harry, "the context of the accident is too simple, and not something likely to cause death."

"We've interviewed the farmer who witnessed the crash and he supports this finding," said François.

"It's confirmed that William was working on a Russian file, a plan to plant Russian operatives to infiltrate significant sectors of government and business," says Rushton. "Sam Carr was a person of interest. We may never know exactly how it happened, and I'm sorry Elizabeth. William Grant's death has now been declared suspicious under duty."

For Elizabeth, this would mean a change in the compensation she received when William died. But Rushton thought it would be in bad taste to bring it up now. It would bring no comfort.

"I should have questioned the circumstances more at the time and not taken everything the police told me at face value," Elizabeth said remorsefully. She got up to get more coffee, but everyone knew she needed a minute to gather herself.

When she sat down again, she said, "What do we know about that Sam Carr and also Kathleen Willsher?"

"Sam Carr is under surveillance, he is known as a "recruiter," says Rushton. "There is also suspicion of Willsher, for trading secrets. She came to Canada in 1930 under a scholarship and found work for the British High Commissioner."

"The thing you must know about them right now is that we are observing, building a case over an extended period. It might take ten years before a trial. We have nothing to arrest them for and don't want to jeopardize the network we are building. You see the spy game is not as glamorous as it appears in movies. It's a web that is built one thread at a time."

"What do you mean by saying that Carr is a recruiter?" asked Peter.

"Russia will plant people in different sectors, government, business. At first, they settle in like anyone else, they will blend in so to speak. Find work, make friends, and be active in the community. Then they start recruiting potential informers. Those informers might be willing, lured by money and power. Others will be reluctant but because of a weakness uncovered by the recruiter they find they have no choice."

"Is that what Josephine Smith did?" asked Harry.

"Yes, especially well-trained beautiful women. They can let men compromise themselves very easily," adds Rushton. "But men recruiters are no better, they find weaknesses in other men, like blondes, booze, homosexuality. It's blackmail after that. Charming gigolos befriend lonely women, asking them to share bits and pieces about their work and next thing they know it's bigger and more dangerous."

"So was Carr trying to recruit William?" asked Elizabeth with a concerned look on her face.

"We don't know, but if they felt they had to get rid of him," said Rushton, "they might have wagered he was a plant, or that he wouldn't go along with it and was a risk."

"I have names for you Frank," said Rushton who

always used the Anglo version of Lefebvre's name. "We have a hub in Montreal and I'll tell you who we are watching."

"Elizabeth, you tell me what Miss Smith has been writing to you," said Rushton.

"First there was her spy novel, a letter and a birthday card," said Elizabeth.

"That was nice of her, the birthday card," smirked John in the background.

"An absolute dear," said Elizabeth. "The birthday card had a cryptic message and a poem. The letter only had a few jumbled letters in a row. I managed to figure the message out as being "SAM CARR UNIONS RUSSIA.""

"Interesting," said Rushton. "That confirms Sam Carr and Russia's involvement, but UNIONS is a new one and a lead into where this is going. The road that the communists will take to infiltrate our society."

"What about the poem?" asked François. "That's odd, more leads?"

"The poem is Shakespeare's "All the World is a Stage," Elizabeth pulled out the card and they passed it around.

All the world's a stage,

And all the men and women merely players;

They have their exits and their entrances;

And one man in his time plays many parts,

His acts being seven ages.

And then the lover,

Sighing like furnace, with a woeful ballad
Made to his mistress' eyebrow.

Then a soldier,
Full of strange oaths, and bearded like the pard,
Jealous in honour, sudden and quick in quarrel,
Seeking the bubble reputation
Even in the cannon's mouth.

"The first verse about all the men and women being players, obviously refers to spies, Josephine herself," said Peter. "The second, the lover, could that be William?"

"The lover in the second verse and the soldier in the third, could be the same person," said Rushton. "We know that Sir Allan Stanfrey is an ex-lover of Josephine and a retired colonel. They met in Ottawa when she was young and he was her recruiter. But for our side. She ended up blackmailing him, so is she scared of him? We know she hates the Russians, she was arrested once, interrogated and exchanged, so no love lost there."

Elizabeth did not comment but she wondered whether Josephine was telling her to fear Stanfrey or to send him the manuscript. Out of the corner of her eye, she noticed Mrs. Denny waving at her. Elizabeth suggested a break for lunch and brought in sandwiches and treats that Mrs. Denny had prepared. Everyone stood up to stretch their legs and had casual conversation. Harry cornered Elizabeth and asked her how she was doing. "It's a lot to take in, isn't it, love?" he said.

After the welcome break they got down to the brass tacks and what to do next.

"Elizabeth, tell me about that other correspondence from Smith," said Rushton, eyes peeled on her, as this was going to be news to most around the table.

"After the case last year, she sent me a manuscript, a memoir of sorts," explained Elizabeth. "It came with a note that said *Keep this safe for me; I trust you to know if and when it might be needed. Josephine Smith.*"

"I'm sorry Edward, but I was tired and done with her, so I put it in my safe and didn't even look at it," she said. "I naively hoped the time would never come…But when she sent me the novel, there was a card that said *The time is now.* I still don't know what it means, I need to look at it and see if the right thing to do is to give the manuscript to the government. This might be a point of contention between you and me, and we are long-time friends, but that's the way it is."

"You are putting me in a difficult situation, my friend," said Rushton. "I will give you some time, to decide but my position is clear if any of it jeopardises national security…"

"Let's take a minute here," said Harry. "If we are talking about memoirs, that would be old stuff, things that happened in the past with people that might be dead now. Will it serve anything that is happening now?"

"Perhaps," said Rushton. "But it's not people as much as governments and countries, foes playing friends. Some of those secrets could shatter diplomacy. Europe is never stable, it's a big chessboard."

"There is another caution here. Since Smith has been corresponding with Elizabeth, they could very well be under some sort of surveillance. They could find out where you are," said Rushton. "You will need to be careful. Remember last year when we made plans, everything was leaked, and it was hard to know whom to trust? The spy web does not only include big names but also clerks and secretaries."

"Perhaps you should move in here," suggested Harry. "There is always someone in the house, you wouldn't be alone."

"Harry, you know I can't do that. I'm in trouble already as it is, with our relationship being too public. I have a meeting scheduled with Father Douglas. I'm a Catholic in 1934 Cornwall and I must give the example, so he says." Elizabeth laughed as she said the words, trying to lighten the mood. "My list of sins is so lengthy and recurring that they've named a confessional after me!"

"Plus, how long do I hide for?" she asked. "I won't let that crazy vengeful woman dictate my life."

"It is Cornwall. What are the odds of anything going on here?" said Rushton.

John got up from his armchair and came to the table. He looked at Rushton and said, "I wouldn't dismiss a risk in Cornwall, Mister Rushton. If we are looking at communist infiltration in trade unions. With three cotton mills employing over 1300, and Courtaulds another 1450, this area represents the largest organization of textile workers in Canada."

"Right you are Mister Warner, and I apologize if

I seem to be minimising the risk," said Rushton. "We have been following the Workers Unity League created in 1930, it has a strong undercurrent of affinity with the Communist Party of Canada and CP International. Last year most of the strikes were led by the WUL."

"We see it here," said Harry. "With the depression, people are not happy with the wages, the working conditions and I can see how a communist party might appeal to them. They might appear to have a better understanding of the issues in the working class."

"Peter, could you talk with your stepfather, he works at Courtaulds," said Elizabeth. "To see how things are there and who are the union leaders."

"In Quebec, there is a large textile and garment industry, with its own unions," said François. "And being in Lachine I'm aware of the Seamen's and Longshoremen Associations. That impacts both the Lachine and Cornwall Canals, they have recurring issues."

"Yes," said Rushton. "In most of Canada, there is a strong American undercurrent in the trade unions. But in Quebec, the unions that formed under the Catholic Church, like the *Confédération des travailleurs catholiques du Canada (CTCC)*, are more autonomous and harder for communists to infiltrate.

"Getting back to making sure we keep Aunt Liz safe; we can figure something out ourselves," said Peter. "Muriel is coming back at the end of the week; someone can stay with you at other times and you can phone at set intervals."

"Yes," she said. "That's a plan." She looked at

Harry who was not happy at all about what he saw as a weak plan. She intended to continue working.

"Harry, put your foot down and have the little woman stay put until this blows over," said Rushton.

They all looked at each other and burst out laughing, knowing full well there was no chance of that ever happening.

Rushton set off to Ottawa, but not before giving Elizabeth a due date for a report about the manuscript. François would go back to Montreal to follow the leads he was handed. There was a call due in a couple of days. Elizabeth and Peter opted to stay for dinner and Julie would come in soon after closing the café. Harry didn't care in the least about what people thought about their relationship and he was going to keep her as close as he could.

Mrs. Denny had left, but not before getting dinner in the oven. They had a drink and Elizabeth was glad to settle into the simple task of setting the table. When Julie came in, they were all glad to move into a lighter discussion about the café and her day.

"Julie, you have to do something about Marcel," said Harry. "He drinks too much coffee! And I think it's because he likes Marianne. He hardly works anymore, he's either getting coffee or in the washroom because he drinks too much and he's hyper from all that caffeine!"

Marcel Chabot was a mechanic at Harry's garage next door. He was in his late thirties, a heavy-set man, with a receding hairline. Julie always saw him as a gentle teddy bear with a large grin and a happy demeanour.

Julie laughed. "What can I do? Can't he ask her out? I don't think she minds him at all, she always wants to be the one taking his order. She giggles like a schoolgirl when he calls her Mademoiselle Marianne!"

"He's too shy. He lived with his mother until she passed away. She never approved of any woman he was ever interested in. So, there you have it, now he's thirty-eight and too scared to make a move," said Harry.

"Peter's the matchmaker here," said Elizabeth. "What do you suggest?"

"How about you say there was a raffle at the garage, two tickets for the movies and Marcel won," grinned Peter. "Now, all you have to do is get that in a conversation, maybe we double date with Marianne and Marcel?"

"You're such a schemer, Peter," said Julie. "But Dad, you know if anything comes out of this my coffee sales are going to go down," said Julie.

"I'll cover any of your losses, so I can have my mechanic working full-time again," laughed Harry.

After dinner, Harry played the piano for a while and John sat beside Elizabeth.

"I know that Harry is worried about you," said John. "Is there a compromise possible? How about you going to my house in Wales? You could work from there, it's private and you can see anyone coming up the drive for miles."

"Perhaps, John," she said. "I could consider it, thank you."

Harry walked her back to her apartment, extending his stay and not leaving before checking all the doors and windows. Elizabeth laughed when he checked the windows, and told him to get a grip, reminding him that she was on the second floor.

Over the next few days, she became smothered by the people in her life. They provided company every minute of the day, and even Dusty the cat felt the need to follow her to the bathroom! Perhaps going to John's house in Wales would be a good idea. She would have a look. A stay in the country might do her good.

Chapter 13

"Yes, Mr. Lefebvre just walked in," said the secretary. "May I know who is calling please?"

"Thank you," she added. "François, there's a call for you, from Muriel."

François picked up the call from his desk. "Hi, how are you doing on this fine morning?" he asked.

"Not so great. I picked up a press release that came in on the wire, she's dead Frank."

"Who's dead? What do you mean?" he questioned.

"I have the copy, I'll read it to you,"

> Saint-Lunaire, France – July 15, 1934 - It is with deep sadness that we announce the untimely demise of esteemed author J.S. Simmons, whose life was tragically cut short in her residence in Saint-Lunaire, France. J.S. Simmons was discovered lifeless in her home on July 14, 1934, leaving the literary community and her devoted readers mourning the loss of an exceptional talent.

Blah…blah…blah…

The circumstances surrounding J.S. Simmons' passing are still under investigation, and authorities are diligently working to uncover the truth.

"I'm worried for my mother," said Muriel. "I tried calling her at home but there is no answer, I'm scared."

"Ok, I will call around, maybe she's with Harry, it's early still. I'll get back to you," said François. "What's your number there?" He took it down. "I will let you know; she might just be out for breakfast or something like that."

François called the office in Cornwall first but there was no answer. It might be too early for Peter to be in. He dialled Harry.

"Hi Harry, it's François, I'm working on something here and I was wondering if Elizabeth is with you," trying not to sound alarming.

"She's gone to Wales with my father," said Harry. "She wanted to get things set up at the house, she may stay there for a while until things cool down a bit. It's only about 20 minutes from Cornwall. You can ring her there if you need."

"It's just that…" started François.

"What? Is anything the matter?" quizzed Harry.

"Well, we've heard that J.S. Simmons, aka Josephine Smith, has been found dead in France," said François. "Can you call me back and confirm Elizabeth is safe? I'm planning to make my way up. I'll give you the number at my place. I'm picking up an overnight bag now."

Harry called his brother who lived up the road from his father's house, but the line was busy. As soon as he put the handset down, it rang…

"Harry, father just came in," said Robert. "He is fine but shaky. Two cars pulled up to them, blocked the road and took Elizabeth."

"Fuck…" Harry exclaimed. "You said father is fine, not hurt?"

"No, he's fine," said Robert. "They pushed him out of the way. He's upset he couldn't stop them. He wants to talk to you."

"Harry, I'm so sorry boy, I couldn't help her," said John. "I hope you can forgive me; they were gone by the time I got up from the fall. But I did see something though, the pickup truck that was in front of us, it stopped and blocked the way before the other car came alongside."

"It's all right Dad, take your time," said Harry. "What about the truck?"

"It was odd because I noticed the licence plate, it was 1933 and we're in 1934," said John. "It was a black GMC pickup, but old and dirty. Looked like a farm truck. I noticed the plate because it had my initials JW and the number, I think was 812, JW 812."

"Thanks, Dad, that could help," said Harry. "When the police get there tell them what you know, ok? Can I talk to Robert again, please?"

"Keep him there," said Harry to his brother. "I have calls to make but have him stay by the phone and I will let you know. The police should be over."

Harry dialled François and informed him of the situation.

"Ok, Harry, stay by the phone at your house, but try to contact Peter," said François. "Muriel called me with the news, so I will call her back. I'll be there in a few hours. We'll figure this out, Harry."

Harry called the garage and spoke with Bob, his head mechanic. He was upset to hear about John and Elizabeth. He asked how he could help.

"Can you look into the repairs we did, for a pickup truck, GMC black, older model, probably used on a farm?" asked Harry. "Listen, Bob, it might be a needle in a haystack but I can't afford not to try this, I'm going out of my mind. My father said the plates were 1933, so maybe we didn't do work on it this year, but maybe parts, the licence plate is JW 812."

"Sure boss, anything," said Bob. "I'll get on that straight away and I will let you know if I find anything."

Harry put down the receiver and paced his living room again.

Peter made his way to the office, coffee and daily paper in hand. He knew that Elizabeth was out to Wales, so he would deal with messages. At the top of the stairs, he noticed the door was ajar, he pushed it open and walked into chaos. The small office was a scene of disarray with books and papers scattered everywhere. Whoever had done this was looking for something, Josephine's memoirs, imagined Peter. One filing cabinet was overturned and rummaged drawers were still open.

In a panic, Peter made his way to Elizabeth's apartment at the back of the property. It was the same there, the kitchen, living room and her bedroom were ransacked. A surge of anger came at Peter, offended that Elizabeth's most private possessions were strewed on the floor, with no regard. He found Dusty scared and hiding behind the refrigerator. He called Harry.

"Harry, something's happened," said Peter. "Elizabeth's apartment and the office have been ransacked, it's a mess."

"It's not good news Peter," confirmed Harry. He told him about the kidnapping, and that François was on his way, so was Muriel.

"I will call Frank Santini from the RCMP," said Peter. "I will stay in the office; we all need to be near a phone so we can update each other."

"I'm going out of my mind Peter," said Harry. "Trying not to imagine the worst. If Santini comes down with RCMP backup, you should send them to the house in Wales. It will attract less attention there and not alert the kidnappers. My brother and father are there to wait for them."

"If they kidnapped her, it means they didn't find the memoirs and might be looking for an exchange," suggested Peter. "It might be our break, Harry. They may reach out to you."

Elizabeth enjoyed the drive to Wales and John was always good company. She had decided to accept his offer to stay at his farmhouse, while things cooled down with this investigation. She didn't pay too much attention when the pickup truck in front of her slowed down, and the car behind moved to pass. She did, however, realize something was wrong when the truck came to a dead stop and the car blocked her in. She had no choice but to stop.

Two men came out of the car. One was wearing blue overalls, a blue shirt with rolled-up sleeves and a grey cap. The windows of her car were rolled down and it was easy to open the doors. She yelled when he grabbed John and pushed him down onto the gravel road. The other one was also wearing the same blue shirt but with blue jeans and wide suspenders. Both had their faces covered with what looked like pillowcases with holes. The owner of the suspenders grabbed Elizabeth.

Kicking and hitting, Elizabeth wasn't going to go easily. She bit the hand of her kidnapper, drawing blood and swear words. Offended, he slapped her hard. Tired of the struggle he finally put a cloth over her mouth and the sweet smell sent her to sleep. He shoved her into the back seat, tying her wrists and ankles as they drove off, leaving John behind. The pickup truck took off right behind them.

"The bitch," he said. "She bit my hand; I'm bleeding for fuck's sake." As he dropped the rope at her feet he ran his hand over her leg, "She's not bad… and feisty like that, I bet she's something…"

"Leave her alone," said the Overalls. "We got enough trouble as it is, we didn't find that stupid book of memories…"

"Memoirs, idiot, memoirs," said the Suspenders. "We've got her, she'll either tell us or those friends of hers will do a trade. There's good money for us in that. We can get a bit extra if her family cares and by the way, that Warner fella, he's loaded."

"I want this over with as quickly as possible," said the Overalls. "Doing a favour and picking up a book is one thing. Kidnapping and who knows what else may come…I'm not interested. She made us run around enough as it is. I'll take her to the farm but I'm no babysitter."

When they took the job, they were told it would be quick and easy. Go to her place, frighten her into giving them the Smith writings and off they would go to collect their fee. But nothing had gone as planned. She wasn't at home, so they tried to find the manuscript themselves, with no luck. Being locals, they knew a bit about her and thought perhaps she might be around Harry's place or his daughter's coffee shoppe. When they drove by, they saw her picking up John Warner so they followed Elizabeth's car.

Chapter 14

Elizabeth opened her eyes and the splitting headache made it hard to focus. She felt a tear in her lower lip and recalled the Suspenders slapping her. Her mouth was dry, she was thirsty. She tried to move but she was stiff and sore in every joint. She was laying on a rusty old metal bed with springs and wires. There was a cut on her calf and she realized she would need a tetanus shot for that. There was nothing between her and the metal base aside from a smelly and prickly horse blanket.

Her hands were tied in front of her but her ankles were free. She tried to sit up and took a deep breath, she turned her head and gagged on the smell of pig excrement, the air heavy and moist with the odours. Elizabeth had a keen sense of smell. She was more likely to remember the smell of an aftershave than a face. She remembered to breathe through her mouth.

A fine stream of daylight pierced through the splits in the wooden boards. She was in a lean-to, next to a pig sty. That she was sure of. When she moved around, the pigs snorted and squealed and it was deafening. Aside from the bed frame, there was a bucket, a few bales of hay, and a few pieces of leather harness. There were no windows and the wooden slats looked sturdy enough, pushing through them would be difficult. The door was bolted from the outside, no luck there either.

She should have been scared, and she was, but her anger overtook other feelings. She tried to remember what she could about her kidnappers but nothing stood out. The Overalls was likely the leader, but neither seemed overly bright. The bottom rung of the criminal ladder rarely was; they were hired hands who knew very little about the bigger scheme. Whoever had organized this, obviously didn't want to spend extra to get brains, only brawn.

By now, the kidnappers had no choice but to set up an exchange for Josephine's manuscript. There was no point trying to get her to tell them where it was, they could never get back in the office. This made her safe for now, she thought. It was a matter of time; she knew that everyone back in Cornwall would be looking for her. How long?

Elizabeth sat on a bale of hay, scrutinizing her surroundings, to see if there was anything she could attempt. She didn't know if Suspenders and Overalls were in the house or if she was alone on the farm. She wished she wore pants like Muriel. Her summer dress was torn and dirty, and it offered no protection. The rope was cutting through the skin of her wrists and she looked for anything that might cut it off. She glanced at the metal bed for any sharp edges she could use. She moved the rope repeatedly over a metal slat but there was nothing to show for the work and she gave up.

She tried to trick her mind into ignoring the pungent smell, thinking of her father's shoe repair shop and the smell of leather. The aroma of good scotch, a nice cigar and Harry's aftershave. She made mental lists of things to do, thought about her grandchildren, and remembered her vacation. Minutes were like hours.

She heard someone at the door, the lock removed and the latch lifted. The noise launched a stint of pig squeals, likely in the hope of being fed. The Suspenders yelled at her to stay where she was and put a cup and a sandwich on the bale of hay beside the door. He left before Elizabeth could say anything and locked the door again. The tea was weak and cold, stale bread covered a thin slice of ham. Elizabeth thought the content of the sandwich might have come from a former resident of this sty, but she was starving and thirsty. Nobody was asking but she would give the service and accommodation here a strong zero-star rating.

As the sun set, she found the most comfortable place to lie down by placing two bales of hay end to end and wrapping herself in the horse blanket. The thin blanket offered no buffer between her skin and the metal wiring if she stayed on the bed. While there was still a shred of light, she went back to running the ropes on her wrist against the metal slat on the bed frame. Within what seemed like hours the rope let go and her hands were free. She wrapped herself in the blanket and brought her legs up. In the dark, she could hear the scratching noises of rats on the wood floor.

Chapter 15

Peter was at a loss in the office and attempted to straighten things out. They would need a decent place to work from. Peter knew the kidnappers had not found the cleverly hidden safe that held the memoirs. Aunt Liz was too smart for that.

François came in, followed an hour later by Muriel. Santini called them to say the RCMP officers had arrived and were talking with John to see if there was anything he could remember that would give them a lead. François called Harry, who was at home alone. He could imagine what Harry was going through.

"Ok, so where is that damn book?" asked François. "Peter?"

"They didn't find the safe," Peter said. "Check the bookshelf that is over the card cabinet. It's attached to the wall. Go to the middle shelf." He showed them.

"It's in nine sections, so check the one right in the centre," Peter directed. "Slide the back panel to the left, and there it is."

"What's the combination?" asked Muriel.

"I don't know," replied Peter. "Elizabeth changed it recently and she thought it would be safer if she was the only one who knew."

"We have to try something, suggestions?" asked François.

"She's strong on dates if I remember previous combinations," said Peter. "Her birthday? 06 13 83?

François tried with no success. Muriel said, "Her father 08 11 44." It didn't work.

Muriel picked up the phone and said, "Harry, when's your birthday? It's to open mother's safe…Ok, thanks." She said to François "Spin that dial to 08 03 84."

And it worked, the lock released and François removed the manilla envelope.

"Muriel, you're the fastest to read through this. Skim it for anything about Cornwall. There might be a name, a line we can pursue," said François. He went over to the desk where she was sitting and before releasing the envelope, he said "I'm giving this to Elizabeth's daughter, not the journalist…that will be for later."

"Yes, sir," she said, worried when she noticed the shoulder holster and gun.

After closing the coffee shoppe at 2 pm, Julie went to sit with her father. He looked dreadful and she felt helpless to do or say anything that could help. Mrs. Denny had supplied him with a flow of coffee and Julie noticed the housekeeper's eyes were red from tears. She had been concerned at the onset of the relationship, that her position would be in jeopardy. Maybe Elizabeth would want things her way, but that had not been the case. Elizabeth had been respectful of her place in the family, after all the years. Mrs. Denny had grown fond of Elizabeth.

Julie decided to pick up Mary and go to Elizabeth's apartment to start straightening up the place. That's all she could do right now, and Muriel would need a clean room. Mary fed the cat and started in the kitchen, while Julie got to work in the bedroom. They worked in silence, there was nothing to say. Julie brought coffee and a few snacks to the office. At 5 pm they had not heard from the kidnappers yet; no demand had been made. She walked back home to her father. She didn't want to leave him alone for the evening. Julie knew Peter and the others would not leave the office.

Harry was crumbling. He looked wretched, but he straightened up when Julie walked in. She told him what the gang back at the office were doing, trying to give him hope. She mentioned that they were able to open the safe because Elizabeth had used his birth date as the combination. Julie said Elizabeth would know he would do everything he could to find her.

Harry skipped a heartbeat when the phone rang.

"Harry, I can't sit by the phone much longer. My bad leg is killing me, I need to move," said François. "Do you want to come with me and rattle a few cages?"

"I would love to," said Harry.

"A name came up when Peter talked to his stepdad," François said. "He was asking about who else in the shop has been leaning towards communism. Do you know Chuck Jones?" François asked.

Bringing Harry along was two-fold. It would give him something to do and being a local businessman, some might be more inclined to talk to him than to a stranger.

"Yes, he's up on Silmser Road," replied Harry. "Pick me up I'm ready. I'll tell Julie to stay by the phone here."

The small white house was north of the tracks, on a small quiet road. They pulled into the drive and it looked like Chuck Jones was at home. He was surprised to see the two men but ushered them into the kitchen.

"What's this visit in aid of Harry?" Jones asked. "The wife is out at bingo, but I have beer if you want."

"No, I'm good, thanks," said Harry. He figured Jones could work the bottle opener but not the kettle. He introduced François as a friend and told Jones they were looking into a break-in at a friend's place.

"Oh, nothing to do with you, directly that is, but your name came up as knowing a few people in the shop union at work," said François. "Maybe some interested in sharing communist ideas, rings a bell?"

Jones leaned back on his kitchen chair and said, "Being part of a union is no crime, and passing on a few leaflets about fairer deals for workers isn't either, as far as I can tell."

"No, it's not," said Harry. "But breaking into an

apartment, ransacking it looking for papers would be. Know anyone beholden to higher-ups for favours, say who might even go to kidnapping? Or anyone looking to hire that sort of help?"

"I think you two better leave now," said Jones. "Might be more trouble for me than it's worth to be seen talking to you."

So, François deduced from that comment that Jones might know more than he was sharing right now. He stood up, took off his jacket and folded methodically shoulder to shoulder and then over. He handed it to Harry.

"Hold this for me please," said François. Jones, who had been balancing on the back legs of his chair, nearly tipped over and the blood drained from his face. He had noticed the gun in the holster.

"What's more trouble now?" asked François. "Me or your friends?"

"You can't scare me, you Frenchie…," said Jones. "Get the fuck out of my house."

"So, who do you know that is getting involved in these things?" asked François moving closer to Jones. "Who's hiring the help?"

Jones made a move for the gun, a stupid move. François kicked the chair and Jones tipped backwards.

"Noticed that I limp a bit?" asked François. "Got shot in the leg, you see. Didn't kill me but it hurt like hell, and now I need a cane when it rains. See what I mean, it's a small thing really, could happen to anyone alone at home cleaning a gun."

"You wouldn't do that, your stupid fuck," said

Jones.

"You know François, it's starting to bother me, the lack of respect and the name-calling," said Harry, cool as he could muster.

"You're right," said François. "And anyway, if it did happen, before you can tell us the names, it wouldn't be me hurting you. How could it, I'm at the movies with my friends right now, aren't I Harry?"

"Ok, Ok, leave me alone," said Jones. "Harold Merkley, the shop steward, was asking for helpers for a job outside work. The dim wit Stan Barker was interested."

"Is this the Barker that lives up on South Branch Road?" asked Harry.

"Yes, it would be him," said Jones.

François put on his jacket and they both thanked Jones for his warm welcome.

Jones muttered "Crazy fuckers" as he locked the door behind them.

Back in the car, Harry and François laughed. "Well, that was an entertaining outing," said Harry.

"Not much we can do right now, but we can check those names against what Peter and Muriel have been doing and we might have a lead worth telling Santini and setting up a visit."

"Thank you," said Harry. It was dark now and they drove in a companionable silence until Harry asked, "Do you have feelings for Elizabeth?"

"This again? Is this all you people talk about around here?" exclaimed François. "Yes, like a sister. I wouldn't stand a chance Harry, she sees only you, and she is not like Maureen. You can trust her."

Maureen had been Harry's wife, famous for her philandering.

"I'm sorry if I'm being an idiot," said Harry.

"I can't blame you, I would probably be asking the same questions," said François. "Actually, my interest might lay elsewhere if I wasn't such an old limping fool."

"I'm worried that the kidnappers haven't called for a ransom, an exchange, anything," said Harry.

"Yes, I know," said François. "But if we think the point of this is to get Josephine's memoirs back they might be waiting for instructions. They need Elizabeth for that to work, but we have names now."

"We will get her back, Harry," said François. "I won't stop. I'm very protective of my sisters you know!"

A single lamp shone a light on the papers on the desk. Muriel could barely focus she was so tired, but she flipped through page after page of Josephine's memoirs. Luckily, the pages were typed and easy to follow with dates and markers. At any other time, the reading would be fascinating, Muriel already noticed details of historical events and figures that could change the way the world perceives them. Josephine Smith had been one impressive woman.

When François and Harry came back, they asked Muriel for an update or calls from anyone. She said all had been silent and there was nothing from Julie or Santini either. Peter was back and getting coffee.

They all compared notes and names, the links were now clear.

"I have a reference, from 1930 about Cornwall's

textile unions, a Harold Merkley, as a Russian plant," said Muriel. "It is one of the last entries from Josephine. The time of my father's work with the communist enquiry."

"I have Merkley and Barker," said Peter.

"We have confirmation of Merkley as well, and Barker that I will send to Santini," said François. "I will call him now. The rest of you should get some rest. We may have an operation in the morning."

Harry offered François a room at his place and told him to come over when he was done with the call. Peter would drop in to see Julie for a few minutes. Muriel had planned to stay at her mother's now that Julie and Mary had cleared some space for her.

François went for the desk phone and ran his fingers over Muriel's forearm, "Good job. You should try to get some rest, you look exhausted." She looked up and tried a faint smile. "I'm all right."

"We will get her back," he said. "You can't stay here by yourself. We are all going to Harry's, so why don't you come and stay with us there?"

Exhausted as they were, they couldn't stand down and relax. Harry made them drinks and finally late in the night he went up to his room, worried sick about Elizabeth. He wondered if she was cold, hungry, or hurt. Sleep would not come easily and when it did nightmares woke him up again.

Muriel fell asleep on the sofa, leaning on François' shoulder. He covered her with a blanket before going to his room.

Chapter 16

It was around 7:30 am when the phone rang at the house. "Harry Warner?" asked the caller with a heavy French accent, so heavy in fact that it sounded like a forced mimic to hide the caller's voice.

"Yes," said Harry.

"We have your girlfriend," said the caller. "We want the Josephine Smith memoirs and $2,000 in cash. No police and no funny business. I like her thick brown hair and she is lovely, would hate anything to happen to her, hear me?"

"Yes," said Harry. "If you touch her in any way, I'll kill you, bastard,"

"Now, now," said the caller. "Nothing rash. Let's meet at noon, that should give you enough time to get the money, and we meet at the north end train station, CNR."

"Wait, can't I get a bit more time, the bank isn't open today. Give me until 1 o'clock," said Harry.

"Ok, but if you're not there at 1 o'clock, it will be wear and tear on the little lady, understand?" said the caller.

"Yes," said Harry. He was relating the conversation to François and Peter when there was a knock at the door. Bob came running in as soon as the door opened.

"Boss, we have something on the pickup truck," said Bob. "It is Norman Simms, lives on South Branch, a pig farmer."

"Great work," said Harry. "François, Simms is the brother-in-law of Barker. They both live on the same road. It's all pointing to them."

Mrs. Denny had made coffee and breakfast for all of them. Only François and Muriel picked up a plate. François called Santini to give him the update. He passed the phone to Harry, so he could tell them where the locations were, and the site specifics for all of them.

"You'd better do it," said François. "I have no clue where South Branch is, even if you told me the farm was between Eamers Corners and Grants Corners!"

The meeting place was the train station, and Santini mentioned that could complicate things. They would plant plainclothes officers, but there would be other travellers and railroad cars to jump into and out of. They made two plans. The first one to investigate the Barker and Simms farms, right now, with François, Peter and the two RCMP agents. The second was to get Harry ready for the 1 p.m. meeting at the train station, should that still be needed after the farm raid. Julie would stay at the house and Muriel at the office, by the phone, to relay any updates to the RCMP dispatch now at John's farm in Wales.

Harry called back and said that Bill at East Side Dairy was willing to loan them a milk truck. They only had to pick it up. It was a good idea and would make it easier to drive up to the farm under less suspicion. Open fields made it harder to sneak up on the kidnappers.

Piece of toast in hand, François put down his coffee and looped his gun holster on his belt. He passed a similar holster to Peter, much to the distress of Julie. "He trained with me in Montreal, Julie. He's quite good, don't worry," said François.

Peter and François made their way to the door, with Harry staying behind to wait for Santini. Julie kissed Peter and, caught up in the moment, Muriel lightly kissed François, to his great surprise. "For good luck," she said.

After picking up the milk truck and meeting the two RCMP officers who would accompany them. They made their way to South Branch Road, north of town. They stopped before the farm and let the two policemen get into the back of the truck.

François drove slowly up the drive and noticed the black pickup and the car by the house. There were a few trees, but otherwise, it was an open field with a barn and a few smaller outbuildings. Peter opened his passenger door but did not walk out in the open, he stayed by the door, using it as a shield. François did the same thing on the driver's side. The officers remained by the back of the truck. All they heard was the squealing of pigs.

Elizabeth knew at the first chance that she would try to escape. Daylight had come, for what seemed to be an eternity and no one came. She was parched and hungry, which did nothing to diminish her anger and her single-mindedness in getting out of this.

Footsteps, a chorus of pig squeals and the tampering of the lock and door made her move to a spot beside the entrance. She was counting on the Suspenders carrying a drink and a plate, so she could push past him. As the door opened, she bolted, he dropped everything but Elizabeth did not know he also had a knife. She could not move fast enough and he grabbed her again, pulled her arm hard and brought her to him.

"Not so fast, you bitch," said the Suspenders. "You think you can run away; you wouldn't even be fast enough. Let the dog out on you, I would."

Elizabeth fought back and he finally grabbed both hands and tied her wrists behind her.

The Suspenders noticed the milk truck in the yard and yelled at the Overalls to come out. François had seen Elizabeth and ran for them. Peter was waiting for anyone coming out of the house, backed up by the policemen. Peter and François had drawn their guns.

"Let her go," François yelled. "It's over, there's no point now, let her go."

The Suspenders, not known to listen to reason, pulled Elizabeth closer to him and put the knife to her throat. Elizabeth could feel her kidnapper against her back and her hands, she signalled

François and he knew she would try something, as dangerous as it was.

Elizabeth grabbed the Suspenders' crotch and squeezed hard, he yelled and bent over just enough for Elizabeth to move left. But he didn't drop the knife. François fired one shot that brought him down. From the corner of his eye, François could see the Overalls, on the porch, rifle in hand, aiming for him. Another shot from behind resonated. Peter had fired before the Overalls could, bringing him down.

Elizabeth ran to François and nearly collapsed. Peter came over with a blanket and wrapped her in it, taking her back to the truck. The RCMP officers took charge, searched the house and called for an ambulance. Both kidnappers were wounded but not dead, so the officers proceeded with the arrest.

They took Elizabeth to the hospital for a check, but she said she was fine, just thirsty and hungry. The nurses looked at the cut on her leg and gave her painkillers and something to help her sleep. Harry arrived at the hospital within minutes of the call he had received, telling him she was safe.

They brought her back to Harry's. They didn't say much, he hugged her, and both were grateful it was over. Harry ran a bath for her and when he saw the bruises on her, his heart broke. He softly washed her hair and made her comfortable in the change of clothes Muriel had brought for her. She lay in bed and he sat in a chair next to her, holding her hand. Elizabeth slept for a while, but woke up with a jump, saying she was going to be sick. The smell of the pigs still filled her nose, she couldn't get rid of it. She asked Harry to come beside her and rested her head on his shoulder, breathing him in.

Chapter 17

Mrs. Denny's solution for what was wrong in the world was always baking. As a stress relief, she baked pies, cookies, buns and cakes. Now that Mrs. Grant was back, she counted on everyone getting their appetite back.

Everyone gathered back at Harry's. Tomorrow there would be reports to file on what happened and Rushton would come down to Cornwall for an update. The atmosphere was subdued, and Peter and François had not said much about the day's confrontation at the farm. They had a quiet dinner; Elizabeth had been sleeping all afternoon and a tray was brought up to her. Harry said she looked better and ate well. They all opted for an early night, except for François who stayed in the living room on his own.

Muriel came down for a midnight snack and heard the creaking sound of the old rocking chair in the dark living room. François was sitting with a drink in hand.

"What are you doing there?" asked Muriel.

"Getting drunk," he replied.

Muriel took the drink out of his hand and sat on his lap, he held her and continued to rock. Her hair smelled of lavender.

"Tell me what happened today," she whispered. And he told her everything, what he feared, what he had done. He couldn't stop talking about other things in the past, what he had seen, and he talked about the darkness. He told her what happened to his leg. That he had been shot by a mobster to set an example so that other cops would stay out of his business. How it had ended his police career and how he still resented it. He made do with the private investigator business but didn't have a clear sense of direction until he partnered with her mother.

Finally, they both fell asleep in the chair. At the first light of day, François sent her to her room.

Peter came to the house early and checked on Elizabeth. She thanked him for rescuing her and told him how proud she was of him. Muriel came down later, wearing a bright summer skirt and white top she had borrowed from Julie.

"This is what it came down to," she said. "I didn't pack much, so I had to borrow from Julie."

"You look very pretty, my dear," said Mrs. Denny as she put a full breakfast plate in front of her.

Muriel noticed that François avoided her eyes and promptly left the dining room to talk to Peter. François had not missed how pretty she looked, her fair hair and those blue-grey eyes, but he remembered all that he had said last night. He had unburdened himself, but now he felt embarrassed by it. He wondered if she would accept it, would he be diminished in her eyes?

Santini and Rushton came in around 10 am. Rushton had brought a box of chocolates for Elizabeth, that went on the sideboard with flowers from the mechanics at Harry's garage.

The familiar scene unfolded with everyone at Harry's dining room table once again. Rushton complimented Mrs. Denny on her plates of sweets, claiming he gained weight every time he came to town. The room fell silent when Elizabeth entered the room. Rushton went to her and took her in his arms, lightly as he thought she might break. Staff Sergeant Santini, who was known for his lack of emotionality, smiled at her and pulled out a chair for her.

"So glad to see you, Mrs. Grant," Santini said. "Great escape I was told. The guys at the office are still talking about how you "squeezed" your way to freedom! One of the guys suggested they call it the "Grant Move" and teach it to recruits in the self-defence class.

That was the longest comment Elizabeth had ever heard out of Santini and everyone laughed. She looked refreshed but was still showing some bruising and a small cut on her lip.

Santini had reports for Peter and François to sign, explaining the use of their firearms and the chain of events. "Luckily, no one died, so it cuts down on the paperwork," said Santini. Peter and François both reflected on that comment. No one died, but no matter the outcome, both had felt an emotional toll. François had fired at a man who held a knife because he thought the kidnapper could hurt Elizabeth. Someone had aimed a rifle at him, and Peter had protected him. For Peter, it had been his first time firing at another human being.

"We've brought everyone in. Simms and Barker are being charged with kidnapping, weapons charges, and everything we can throw at them. Merkley, who hired them is also being brought in. We want to find out more about the link between communists and unions here in Cornwall. Maybe leading to bigger fish in Canada."

"I would like to thank everyone for finding me and getting me out of there," said Elizabeth. Looking at Rushton, she added, "I will give Josephine Smith's memoirs to you, Edward."

"I appreciate that Elizabeth, thanks," said Rushton.

"Peter will take you to the office and you can take it back with you. I didn't want to risk walking around the streets with it myself," said Elizabeth.

"I would like to say that it's over," said Rushton, "but we all know better. There are still unanswered questions. Hopefully with no need for you, Elizabeth, to be directly involved, only follow-ups on what we know."

"Thank you for that," said Harry.

Peter and Rushton left to go pick up the manuscript. François went to get his bag, but he stopped for a cookie on his way to the door. He promised to take it easy for a few days and follow up with Elizabeth and Peter next week about other cases they had left pending. He saw that Muriel was sitting on the veranda. He saw Peter and Rushton come back and rush into the house again. He followed them inside; they went directly to Elizabeth.

"While I was in the office, I had a look through the mail and there is something you might want to see," Peter said as he handed Elizabeth an airmail envelope.

"It's from J.S. Simmons again," said Elizabeth. "Dated July 13th, the day before she died!"

Harry thought, "Here we go again"…and he asked, "More coffee, anyone?"

One sheet with the scribbled handwriting of the coded words Yzgtlxke Gtzutub zxgozuxy was all it contained.

"It's the same cypher again, let me get my alphabet workbook," said Elizabeth.

"Based on the original code this would say 'Stanfrey Antonov traitors' I believe. She is confirming the involvement of Colonel Stanfrey, the man who was her lover and that she blackmailed," said Elizabeth.

"We know him," said Rushton. "But he is British with MI6 secret service. Antonov I will need to investigate. Can I take all of this?"

"Absolutely, be my guest," exclaimed Elizabeth.

Rushton collected everything and told her he would call next week with his findings.

There was another, hopefully, final round of goodbyes. François picked up his bag again.

Muriel was sitting outside and said goodbye to Santini and Rushton. She had not been allowed anywhere near that meeting given her work at a major newspaper. François came out and dropped his bag to sit beside her.

"So, the manuscript is gone? There goes my chance for a Pulitzer," she sighed.

"Perhaps, but there might be something you could do," smiled François. "You had a glimpse into a private and mysterious world, perhaps you could write about it. If Josephine Smith can write a bestseller, I'm sure you can as well."

"You think?" asked Muriel with some excitement. "I wouldn't give up my day job, but I could expand my work…Not a bad idea."

"You could make it about a female private investigator, or a policewoman. Tell your readers about the challenges," continued François.

"Yes, a whole chapter on uniforms and pockets," she laughed. "I could write in some romance maybe. The lead character could fall in love with a handsome older detective, something along those lines."

"Those storylines don't always work out you know," he said as he got up and picked up his bag. As a goodbye, he kissed her cheek. Muriel had enough of the older brother's routine and kissed him on the lips. The sort of kiss you could lose yourself in, not minding that they were on a veranda on the main street. He kissed her back but finally pulled away and went to his car.

François had gotten in his car quickly, making a clean break but he couldn't escape the voice in his head. It wouldn't let this go. It berated him for being so stupid. "What are you doing man? You're a disgrace, Lefebvre! I wish I was someone's else voice in their head. Go ahead run away. Tell yourself it won't work."

"Oh, shut up," said François, wishing he had a car radio to distract his mind. But the rant did not subside. "Do you have to have everything figured out? Beginning to end, can't you take a chance? What are you going to do, sit on the fence and look backwards for the rest of your life? You've talked to her more than to anyone, ever, and she listened. She gets you. Didn't you feel that kiss?"

On the steps of the veranda, Muriel was resigned. It is what it is, she thought. She felt they had a connection, perhaps she had been wrong. As she got up to go back into the house, she saw a black car slow down by the curb. It stopped, the window rolled down and François said, "How about Chinese Food?" he asked.

"Give me a minute," she ran into the house to get her bag.

Elizabeth came into the kitchen and asked Mrs. Denny if she had seen Muriel.

"Yes, she just ran out, she said she was going for Chinese Food in Montreal," she said. "In Montreal! I don't know why she'd do that; we have perfectly good Chinese here in town!"

Elizabeth smiled, she knew there was more to the attraction than just Chinatown. Did she approve? She didn't have to, but she thought they might be good for each other. François could use a bit of exuberance in his life and Muriel could do well with someone supportive and mature. Elizabeth would have to thank Santini for suggesting that

François and she could work together. She had needed more experience in investigative work, but not from someone overbearing or who would not have taken her seriously. In that regard, François had been the ideal partner. In return, the rigour and the importance she placed on the work had given him a sense of pride. Although he had been successful with his agency, he had considered this second career as a poor substitute for his ambition in the police force. Now, he knew it didn't have to be that way.

Their partnership was best exemplified by the respective names of their offices: *Grant & Lefebvre* in Cornwall and *Lefebvre & Grant* in Lachine/Montreal.

Mary dropped by Harry's to pick up Elizabeth for a visit to her apartment. She had not been there since the break-in. They had put things back in place, the best they could, but some of her personal items had been broken. Elizabeth also missed Dusty the cat. The office was fine, but her apartment did not feel like her home anymore. Something more than knick-knacks had been broken. Mary made her tea, given there was little else in the cupboards and no milk. They sat for a while at the kitchen table.

"You know Mary," started Elizabeth. "I had some time to think, while I was listening to the pigs and I was wondering if I have been fair to Harry."

"What do you mean?" asked Mary.

"The relationship has always been on my terms, my reticence to commit, my freedom," Elizabeth said. "He took what I gave and never asked for anything. And me, I'm killing him with worries. Will he ever get tired of my antics?"

"I think he knows that's part of who you are," said Mary. "A big reason why he loves you. He did choose you you know. I don't think he would be in this relationship if he didn't want to be."

"You're right," said Elizabeth. "Dark imaginings when you have that much time on your hands, it was bleak. I imagined all the widows and spinsters in town lining up to ask him out!"

"So, what are you doing next?" asked Mary.

"I'm thinking about it, I have a few ideas," Elizabeth laughed.

"Do you have Muriel's number?" asked Mary. "I need to tell her about the letter we sent out and the positive outcome.

"Tell me how it's going. Any hope in getting support for a new agency?" Elizabeth asked.

"It is good news, and in great part, thanks to the article Muriel wrote," said Mary. "I believe the impact had been better than if it had only been published in the paper. The direct solicitation for support has been strong."

"We will need to present to Council when they start back in September, of course," continued Mary. "But informally I have been told it will get support."

"In what form?" asked Elizabeth, "How long will it take?"

"As you know, in government, even municipal government, nothing is quick," laughed Mary. "But we should be able to get Mayor Horovitz to request a community study from The Canadian Welfare Councill in Ottawa. They could start in the fall and report early next year. Charlotte Whitton is the executive of the council. I know her from my work with the Victorian Order of Nurses, the VON."

"Not just another report, I hope," said Elizabeth.

"No, they will look at Health Services, Housing, Family and Welfare Relief, Child Care and Protection, even Recreation," explained Mary. "This report will lend credibility to our findings; their recommendations will likely lead to changes. It will be hard to ignore."

"It's exciting," said Elizabeth. "Muriel will be pleased."

"So, you're coming back to work next week, I imagine," said Mary. "When are you moving back to the apartment?"

"Tonight, now that I'm safe again," said Elizabeth. "You know I can't stay at Harry's."

"Do you think that Josephine Smith is truly dead?" asked Mary. "She keeps bouncing back like the cat with nine lives and to tell you the truth, I don't even trust her to be dead!"

"Rushton will look into it," said Elizabeth as she tried to sound confident but her eyes betrayed a worry. "They must have a body and have been able to identify her, I'm not sure how she died."

"She was in Saint-Lunaire right?" asked Mary. "Did I ever tell you that I was there in 1923?"

"No, I always wondered why Josephine chose it for her retirement, however brief that was," said Elizabeth.

"It's a wonderful place, in Brittany, a northern seaside resort," said Mary. "They call the area the

Emerald Coast. It has a large casino hotel and is visited by crowned heads, businessmen and artists of all sorts. Painters and writers would gather in the cafés, you never knew who you could meet there."

"Why had you gone there?" asked Elizabeth. She was always curious about Mary's life before she came back to Cornwall after her father's death. She felt there was more left unsaid.

"I was in between art classes, I had been in France and after Saint-Lunaire, I came back to Montreal and took more classes and entered my work in exhibitions. And the rest is history as they say."

Chapter 18

Sunday evening Elizabeth moved back into her small apartment. Harry helped her bring back her clothes and the paperwork she had kept at his place. Early that afternoon they had picked up John from the farmhouse. He still felt embarrassed that he had not been able to defend her against the kidnappers. Elizabeth comforted him and said there wasn't much anyone could have done at the time. It was all behind them now.

With groceries done, and shelves and refrigerator stocked again, she was ready, or so she thought, to get back to her routine. Harry was sulking over the move, and of course, he stayed with her the entire evening. Most pleased with this return to certain normality was Dusty the cat. When Harry left, Elizabeth wrapped herself and Dusty with the quilt that had been her birthday present.

The stack of mail, bills to be paid, messages to return and work bookings were a welcome back greeting that sobered her Monday morning. She grabbed a second cup of coffee and waited for Peter.

Together they poured over the agenda and decided on the priorities. François had asked if Peter could go to his Lachine office and work with him for the next two weeks. He needed to get ahead on the leads Santini and Rushton had given him. Irene, his part-time help would look after his other cases. Rushton also phoned to say it would be a while before he could tell her more about their investigation into Smith, Stanfrey and communist infiltration.

Elizabeth still had the occasional nightmare about being kidnapped, the smell coming back to her, and the pig squeals waking her up in fright. Occasionally she needed to take a deep breath. She went for walks on the waterfront and Central Park where she often sat with Marianne. She even went to the library just to smell books; she loved the smell of new books and the crackling sound that comes from the fold of a new spine. Only the head librarian understood that quirk of hers.

There was more time spent on socializing, back to her charity work and teas with Mary. She picked up Harry for lunch most days and they went to Julie's coffee shoppe.

"Look at the counter," said Harry. "That's Marcel, my mechanic, coming in for yet another coffee!"

There was a line-up, and the first in the queue was a short and bulky man, who had no patience. Marianne came to the front counter to help and the man seemed to recognise her. Was it terror or embarrassment that came into her eyes? thought Elizabeth.

"Hey Annie, if it isn't little Annie?" said the man.

But Marianne was trying hard to blend into the background. "Don't you recognise me, from Clark Street, Red Light? I know you, Christ, half of Montreal knows you!"

By now, the whole café was looking at the scene and Elizabeth felt bad for Marianne, she didn't deserve this.

Marcel stepped in and said, "Excuse me, but Miss Marianne, does not seem to know you, you might be mistaken. She has been a friend of mine for a while and she is Marianne not that Annie you claim to know."

"Mind your own business, you Frenchie," said the man as he turned around and raised his fist to Marcel.

"Hey, Bob, open the door, I need to take out the trash," said Marcel, as he grabbed the man's fist in his large paw, twisted it around and grabbed him by the collar. He pushed him out the door and said, "I don't like being called Frenchie."

Everyone in the café applauded and then went back to their meals. Marianne blushed and whispered "Thank you" to Marcel. Julie said he was getting free coffee and moved him ahead of the line.

"Marcel, I hear you won some movie tickets, at the garage," said Julie.

"Yes, I won two tickets, I was lucky," he said.

"Do you have any plans to use them?" asked Julie.

"No, not yet. I did win two though," said Marcel looking at Marianne.

"This Saturday, we're going to see *The Red Rider,*

a western at the Capitol," said Julie. "Would you like to come with Peter and me?"

"That could be fun, I love westerns, but I did win two tickets… do you think Marianne might come with us?" he asked hopefully.

"Marianne, do you want to come to the movies with us?" asked Julie. "Marcel won tickets in the garage raffle."

Marcel held his breath for so long, anxiously waiting for an answer that he was turning blue at the edges.

"Sure, that would be nice," finally said Marianne. "I haven't been to the cinema here and I only went once before."

"All right," smiled Marcel. "Saturday, I will pick you up at 6:30 pm and we will meet Peter and Julie at the Capitol Theatre."

Harry who had witnessed the exchange said "That's my girl, she did it! I bet he's going to put in a good day's work now."

As promised, Marcel picked up Marianne and they walked up to the Capitol on Second Street. Marianne had never seen such a beautiful movie theatre, with a large lobby, sconces in the form of seashells and plaster figures all around. It was a large theatre but always full, especially on weekends. They met Julie and Peter at the concession stand. Marcel got drinks and popcorn for everyone, saying it made up for the free tickets he'd won. He was shy but his intentions were sweet. Marianne grew more trusting and comfortable as the evening progressed.

Marcel walked Marianne home after the movie

and he asked if he could kiss her, on the cheek, of course. She said yes, but she had wanted and proceeded to tell him more about herself, and what she had done in the past. Prostitution was not something most men would ignore and she had seen just recently how someone could recognize her. She couldn't dismiss it. She said she would understand if he didn't want to see her again. Marcel listened to her and asked, "Did you love any of the men, did you want to be with them?"

"No," replied Marianne.

Marcel had a simple way of looking at things. All his life his mother had told him the women he knew weren't good enough for him. Now, at thirty-eight, he was lonely and his house was empty. He was drawn to Marianne in a way he couldn't explain. Perhaps she needed a big guy like him to look out for her.

"Marianne, do you think you could come to like someone like me?

"Yes, I could," she said. And she knew that it was true. More than anyone, he had shown her tenderness.

"I never knew Annie, but I know Marianne," he said. "Do you want to go for a drive tomorrow? Have you ever seen the Rapids? We could stop in Moulinette at Matthew Campbell's for ice cream and go see them."

"That would be lovely," replied Marianne and she kissed him on the cheek.

Marcel walked away humming, thinking he might have a girlfriend! He would have to tell Harry.

Rushton had been in meetings most of the week, reports had come in, and higher-ups were getting involved. What was coming out of this investigation would require finesse and international diplomacy. Past a certain point, it was above his pay grade and sometimes even his security clearance. The RCMP and his department would continue the surveillance of the communist involvement in the trade unions. They had names, and all they had to do would be to wait until the web was complete. It was long-term planning.

Internationally though, it was geopolitics at its best. Josephine Smith was a Canadian by birth, living in France, supported by the British. She had previously been working with the Irish and everyone was eyeing the Russians. Nobody was forgetting that Adolph Hitler had been elected Chancellor of Germany in January 1933.

A phone call to wrap things up was originally planned but now Rushton saw that it just wouldn't do, a face-to-face was needed. He scheduled a meeting with Elizabeth, Peter and François for the following Friday. There was some significance to the choice of day, the last day before a weekend would give everyone some time to regroup. He would also bring his wife with him, she could shop during the meeting and afterwards, they could do dinner and stay for the weekend. He had put in a lot of long hours for this case and a nice break was due.

François drove Peter back after having worked together all week on the links they had found in Montreal's trade unions. They had a file for Rushton.

Peter came in first, saying that François was at Julie's, catching up with Marianne.

"So, you had a good week?" asked Elizabeth.

"Yes, I did, I stayed at François', but honestly I don't know if I can take another day of him telling me how wonderful Muriel is!" laughed Peter. "It's probably payback for me doing the same about Julie."

"I'm glad he is happy, I know that Muriel has been submitting articles about the arrests that were made public," said Elizabeth. "She is coming down from Ottawa by train, at the end of the day."

"Do you think we are all having dinner together?" asked Elizabeth. "Edward is bringing his wife; will it be the old folks on one side and the younger set on the other?"

"I don't know," said Peter. "We can talk about it; I don't mind either way. I have been friends with Harry longer than you have known him. I used to go to his garage with my father. I was just a kid but he always took the time to talk to me. After my father passed away, I dropped in once in a while and talked."

"Good thing you are friends," said Elizabeth. "Especially now that you are seeing his daughter!"

"About that..." started Peter. "I'm sorry about the other day when we dropped in to feed the cat and you came in when we...It's just that one thing led to another and..."

"It's ok Peter," said Elizabeth. "I understand, but I think you and Julie need to see what's next and talk, maybe talk to Harry."

"You're right about that," said Peter, just as François came in with coffee for everyone.

This time they opted to meet in her office, and Rushton came in after lunch. He told Elizabeth about bringing his wife, Juliet, and their plans for the weekend. Elizabeth knew Juliet from her time in Ottawa when both their husbands had worked together. She liked her but for some unknown reason, they had never become more than acquaintances. Juliet's conversation always revolved around her children, the house and cooking.

"My wife is out shopping while we have this meeting," said Rushton. "Hopefully there will be money left to pay for dinner!"

"It's good of her to support the local economy," laughed Elizabeth.

"I'm sure you are all eager to see where we are in this investigation," said Rushton. He explained that some things they could conclude and close, and others would remain under ongoing investigations. As far as Elizabeth was concerned, with Josephine Smith's memoirs now held by Ottawa, her name and visibility were removed.

"With the last message that she sent, the Stanfrey Antonov Traitors script, we were led back to Saint-Lunaire, her last known address."

He continues, "She settled there and as you may know, Saint-Lunaire is a resort with a casino, hotels, and a hub for international visitors. Artists like to sojourn there, very cosmopolitan. There she meets Sergei Antonov, a Russian writer. They might have met before but they hit it off, and over pillow talk the name of Alan Stanfrey is mentioned."

"The British MI6 agent, the love of her life," said Elizabeth. "Minus the bribery and betrayal."

"No couple is perfect, Elizabeth," said Rushton.

"At some point in her career, Smith had been held and interrogated by the Russians, and there was a prisoner exchange, arranged by Stanfrey," said Rushton. "So Antonov lets it drop that Stanfrey had been the one who led the Russian to her in the first place. It seems he was playing both sides, a double agent in a high-ranking position."

"So that's why she came out of retirement," said Elizabeth. "Plain old revenge!"

"That's always a motivator," said François. "It works well with love and greed."

"Long story short, she writes to you and leaks Stanfrey's name," said Rushton. "But Stanfrey is not one to lose sight of the prize, so he keeps a tab on her, and it leads him to you. Through their communist operatives in Canada, they use Cornwall's assets to try and get that manuscript back. He had been looking for it all along. She used it to blackmail him, but she had refused to tell him who had it."

"So, is she dead?" asked Elizabeth, a puzzled look on her face.

"Not exactly," hesitates Rushton.

"What the F…." says François as they all look at each other.

"What is 'not exactly'?" asks Elizabeth. "Death is sort of an absolute, you are or you are not!"

"The thing is…" starts Rushton. "The circumstances are somewhat shady. We have a body, but it can't be identified with any conclusion."

"What's a body that cannot be identified?" asked Peter.

"Burnt," said François.

"Exactly," replied Rushton. "It is her house, or rather her garden shed, which held fuel, cleaning fluids, the whole lot. Burned to the ground, with a body in it. Burnt beyond recognition. It's early days for dental recognition, she never saw a dentist in France and there are jurisdiction challenges. Will we ever know?"

"I knew it," said Elizabeth. "I can't even trust that woman to be dead!"

"We expect that's it's over though," said Rushton. "On a personal level, Smith got what she wanted. Stanfrey is being handled by the British. You don't have her memoirs anymore, it's in the Canadian government's hands. Her only worry should be that the Russians will be on the lookout for her, revenge works both ways. So you should be out of their sight, Elizabeth."

"I hope so," said Elizabeth, with Peter and François nodding in accord. "Good, let us move on." Elizabeth tried to sound cheerful, but they all knew it was more hope than certainty.

"Are you having dinner with us, Edward?" asked Elizabeth. "What are everyone else's plans? Muriel should be coming in with the 6 p.m. train from Ottawa. I can book us a table somewhere, any preference?"

Elizabeth checked with Harry and John would join them with his friend Ruby.

"A table for ten, where?" asked Elizabeth.

"Why don't you try Duncan MacDonald's next door to Julie's café," said Harry. "It might be nice to give him some business back, he was good about Julie opening up her restaurant next to his."

"Great idea," said Elizabeth. "Muriel is coming in on the 6 p.m. train, so I will book for 6:30."

Duncan was more than happy to get the business. He would set up a section for them and Elizabeth booked under the name Warner family.

It was a lively evening, with plenty of teasing and varied conversation. Muriel had not seen Juliet and Edward Rushton for years. She had gone to school with their children and they enjoyed catching up. Everyone avoided any shop talk, but Elizabeth knew that Harry would be curious to find out any outcome. He may not be thrilled with some of the news, but that would be a conversation to be had much later.

Harry asked François what his plans were for the weekend and John answered for him.

"He's been recruited as a farm hand!" laughed John.

"Turns out he's never been to a working farm," said Muriel. "Your brother Robert is haying, so we are going for a visit, and a picnic by Hoople's Creek."

"I grew up in Montreal's east end," said François. "The only grass we saw grew between the cracks in the sidewalk. Robert is loaning me coveralls, boots, the whole lot!"

Peter suggested they drop by with a camera. The older folks left after dinner; the younger crowd stayed a bit longer. Duncan didn't mind, everything was cleared and cleaned, and it was more of a private party now.

Conclusion

"What are you looking at?" asked Elizabeth as she noticed Harry going through the *For Sale* ads.

"It's just a thought, but remember on our vacation, we had a great time at the cottage on the lake," said Harry. "Perhaps we should buy one, not as grand as Edgar's and not that far, but you and me, together."

"Not a bad idea, actually," said Elizabeth. "What are you thinking when you say 'you and me'?"

"Well, right now it's *my* and *your* apartment," noted Harry. "This would be something we could get together; it would be *ours.*

"Move over," as she leaned in the newspaper. "Where?"

"Maybe something within easy reach of Cornwall and Ottawa. Not too much of a drive and the kids could enjoy it too," said Harry. "I know the river is nice, but I would prefer a lake with a small beach."

"And who gets the boat? Am I right in thinking you would like a boat to go with that?" asked Elizabeth.

"As a matter of fact," smiled Harry. "I heard from Edgar. He invited *me* and a strong emphasis on *you*, to one of his summer parties. Which by the way, we are <u>not</u> going to…but he did say he was putting his runabout up for sale. That got me thinking…"

"Could we have a word?" asked Peter. Harry looked up from the paper. Julie sat beside Elizabeth on the sofa but Peter remained standing, awkwardly pacing at the end of the coffee table.

"What's up?" asked Harry.

"Julie and me…Julie and I, well, Elizabeth said we should come and talk to you," stammered Peter.

"Get it out," said Harry.

"You see, we have been friends for over a year now and we get along really well, best friends really," Peter continued. "And we talked about it and what looks like the sensible next step. We discussed waiting a bit for children and Julie continuing to work and I'm all for that, so logically…"

"Yes?" said Harry, trying not to smile and embarrass him further.

"So, we thought, that I should come over and ask you for her hand in marriage," exhaled Peter.

"And how does my daughter Julie feel about this?" asked Harry glancing over at Julie.

"You know my life has been a little complicated before I came here," she said. "But Peter has always been there and he's helped me with the restaurant and we get along well. So it's only natural that…"

"Julie, do you love him?" asked Harry.

"A lot," says Julie.

"Ok, so let me see," said Harry. "Peter, do you

have good career prospects to be able to support my daughter?"

Peter was fidgeting and worried but he said, "Yes, I do Harry. I have a decent income and I was able to pay back my car loan and I have been living on my own now paying rent."

"And what about a house or an apartment, can you afford somewhere decent for my daughter and future grandchildren to live in?" Harry enquired.

"Elizabeth said she could let us use her place to start," said Peter. He was starting to sweat and looked at Julie.

Harry glanced at Elizabeth; he didn't remember her mentioning moving.

"Harry, stop it," laughed Elizabeth. "Stop giving Peter a hard time."

Harry laughed, "I would be happy to have you as my son-in-law Peter."

There were hugs all around and Peter and Julie looking relieved went to sit outside and talk.

"Why the frown?" asked Elizabeth. "They're good together, you know that."

"It just seems all too 'logical', he said they were best friends, which is a good base for a marriage but is it the 'logical next step'? Are they in love, is there passion? I don't want either of them to settle because it's rational."

"I caught them together in my apartment, so I don't think you have to worry about that side of it," laughed Elizabeth. "That's why I told them to come and see you."

"There is one thing though, I'm wondering how

they will deal with the religious aspect of this marriage?" said Elizabeth.

"What do you mean?" said Harry. "Because he is Catholic and she is Protestant? She comes with me to St. Paul's United Church."

"Yes, just curious to see where they go, that's all," said Elizabeth. "I wonder what his mother will say."

"So, what's this about them getting your apartment?" asked Harry. "You never said anything about moving."

"No, it's something else," she said. "You know while I was kidnapped, I had time to think and I came to the conclusion that if you asked me to marry you, I wouldn't say no."

"That's good to know," said Harry as he picked up his cup and went to the kitchen.

Elizabeth followed him. "Well?" she said.

"Well, what? Are you asking me to marry you?" asked Harry.

"No, it's the man that's supposed to ask. So?" she replied.

"Is this your one concession to traditional roles, that the man should ask the woman if she wants to marry him? That being the case then, maybe, just maybe, you want to let the man pick the best place and time to propose, no?" commented Harry.

"Maybe, but…" she said.

"Plus, I may need to think about this," he said. "As it stands, because of your lack of regard for propriety, I get a fair amount of fringe benefits from this relationship already without the 'burden' of the legalities. See what I mean?"

"I see the debate, but…" said Elizabeth. "But depending on the outcome of this conversation, there could be more or less of the fringe benefits in your future."

"Are we resorting to bribery?" he laughed out loud. "Good to know," he said and he walked back to the living room.

"Mrs. Denny," Harry called out to his housekeeper.

She came into the living room and was rather surprised that Harry had called her in such a manner.

"I'm sorry Mrs. Denny. I didn't mean to shout, but do you still have that thing I gave you for safekeeping?" he asked.

She went back into the kitchen and gave Harry a small black box. She had a wide grin on her face and looked pleased by this request.

"I told Mrs. Denny to hide this for me. I couldn't risk anyone finding it before it was time," said Harry as he opened the velvet box and showed the distinct-looking engagement ring. It was white gold, with beautiful scrollwork and filigree on the ring. The solitaire centre diamond was elevated and stood out by its brilliance.

"Will you marry me?" Harry asked.

"Yes. I would be honoured to," said Elizabeth.

Mrs. Denny clapped and cheered loud enough that Peter and Julie came running in from the front veranda, John came down from his room. The worried look faded when Elizabeth flashed her ring.

"Finally," they said in unison.

Ginette Guy Mayer

Photos

Elizabeth thought you might be curious about some of the things and places mentioned in her investigation. She wanted to share with you her photos to provide extra background to this case.

We hope you enjoy them,

Ginette Guy Mayer on behalf of

Elizabeth Grant

1- Example of sub-standard housing during the 1930s housing crisis in Cornwall. The reason behind Elizabeth, Mary and Muriel's involvement in making improvements.

2- Cottage on Lake Simcoe where Elizabeth and Harry stayed during their vacation. It was loaned to them from his friend Edgar.

3- Fountain at Central Park with bandshell in the background.

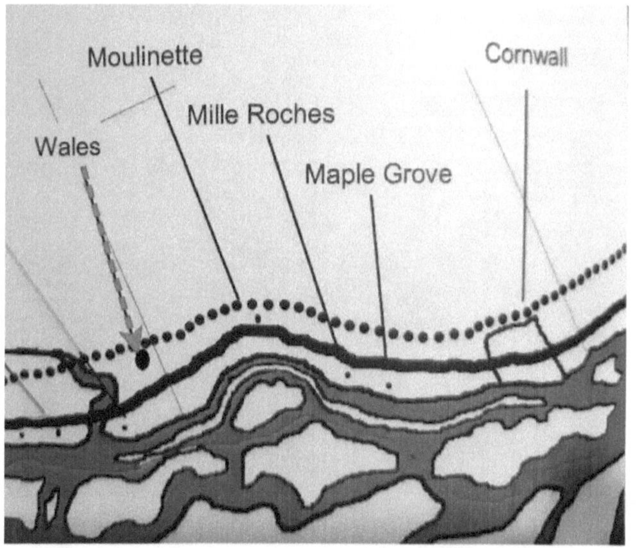

4- Map showing the location of Wales, the Warner's hometown. It was about 20 minutes drive from Cornwall.

5- Cattle and horse barn with granary and pig pen lean-to.

6- Elizabeth's engagement ring. Known as the Elizabeth Solitaire this ring is vintage inspired. The centre solitaire diamond is raised to allow maximum light and brilliance.

Photo Credits

1- House in Cornwall during housing crises, c. 1930, Cornwall Community Museum

2-Cottage on Muskoka Lake is used as an example of the cottage Elizabeth and Harry stayed at during their vacation. Muskoka Lakes, ON Source LAC PA-067357|3317948 Date=circa 1908 Author creator: Frank W. Miclethwaite Permission=Copyright expired. As a pre-1946 Canadian image, also public domain.

3- Water Fountain, Central Park, Cornwall from the Postcard collection of Lilly Worrall, c. 1900 http://www.cornwallpostcards.ca/parks-militaria.html

4-Map showing the location of Wales, west of Cornwall. Esso Road Map 1934, Lost Villages Historical Society Collection

5- 1916 Cattle and horse barn with granary and pig pen lean-to, University of Wisconsin Madison, ca 1976

6- Diamond Engagement Ring – Elizabeth Solitaire from Soha Diamond Company www.sohadiamondco.com/

Books are treasures to be shared

To view other books in this series or to keep track of new projects you can visit my website
www.ginetteguymayer.com

www.ingramcontent.com/pod-product-compliance
Lightning Source LLC
Chambersburg PA
CBHW031332060726
47590CB00007B/2438